EMBASSY OF THE DEAD

DESTINY CALLING

Will Mabbitt

With illustrations by
Chris Mould

Orion
Children's Books

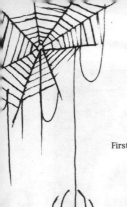

ORION CHILDREN'S BOOKS

First published in Great Britain in 2020 by Hodder and Stoughton

1 3 5 7 9 10 8 6 4 2

A CIP catalogue record for this book
is available from the British Library.

ISBN 978-1-5101-0459-4

Printed and bound in Great Britain by Clays Ltd, Elcograf S.p.A.

The paper and board used in this book are made
rom wood from responsible sources.

Orion Children's Books
An imprint of
Hachette Children's Group
Part of Hodder and Stoughton
Carmelite House
50 Victoria Embankment
London EC4Y 0DZ

An Hachette UK Company
www.hachette.co.uk www.hachettechildrens.co.uk

For Dad

EARLY MORNING VISITORS

Zorro the fox had died of sadness, curled around the broken body of his beloved owner. He was happier now - as a ghost - rooting around in the quiet of the night behind the wheelie bins at the end of the lane. He knew that at any time he could turn around and trot back up to the house, fade through the wall and curl up at the foot of his new master's sleeping bag. He looked up at the sound of a breaking twig. A human had appeared. A lady - dressed in a shabby, grey dress - was standing watching the farm. His master's territory.

Zorro's nose twitched. By her side, nearly invisible in the moonlight, was another woman. Almost identical - a little younger perhaps - but sharing the same hawk-like, pinched features. The older woman stood hunched against the cold night, but this

1

younger one seemed oblivious to its chill. She turned and nodded to what was surely her sister, and with that small movement she faded slightly, her hair merging with the darkness like threads spun from the night itself. Zorro pressed himself into the shadow of the bins, for she, like him, was a ghost, and strange ghosts usually meant danger. The two women started to walk towards his master's house, eventually disappearing into the darkness. Ignoring the tantalising scent of yesterday's chicken dinner in the nearest wheelie bin, he turned and soundlessly padded after the sinister pair.

Zorro watched from the edge of the farmyard as the ghost sister faded effortlessly through the bolted door of the cottage. He preferred to slink through the closed glass door, and this he did, appearing in the small gap between the refrigerator and the wall.

Across the room, the boy was cocooned in a sleeping bag on the sofa. From upstairs Zorro could hear the sound of snoring. His master's father? One of those that couldn't see him. A window in the kitchen was ajar, and the ghost signalled to her sister outside, pointing to the gap.

Her sister's long and bony arm reached in and undid the latch for the main window. There was a slight click and the ghost glanced at the bulging sleeping bag, seeming relieved to see no movement from the child safely tucked inside.

Dead to the world.

The ghost giggled as her older sister clambered in through the window.

'You do look funny, Agnes,' she said teasingly. 'A very unlikely cat burglar!'

The older sister scowled as she climbed carefully down from the kitchen side. 'Hush! Stop playing the fool, Nancy. We have work to do.'

The living sister, Agnes, reached into the folds of her dress. There was a flash of silver in the moonlight and the smirk fell from Nancy's lips as she saw the knife in her sister's hands. Zorro tensed, the fur on the back of his neck lifting.

'Darling Agnes, is this really necessary?'

Her sister nodded. 'I'm afraid it is, dear Nancy.'

Her hand reached out for the sleeping bag, and gently began to peel it backwards.

Slowly . . .

3

Zorro sniffed the air.

Slowly . . .

He had smelt something.

Slowly . . .

Or rather he'd smelt the *absence* of something.

Agnes paused, then whipped the sleeping bag from the sofa. There was no boy, only pillows.

It was as Zorro had thought. The boy's unique scent was old. He wasn't in the sleeping bag. He wasn't even in the house.

The older sister cursed and looked at the younger, who clapped her hands together with relief. 'The Wormling lives to fight another day! I was rather rooting for him.'

The older sister frowned. 'It's not a game, Nancy.' Her eyes narrowed. 'Besides, there is more than one way to skin a rat.'

An excited smile spread across Nancy's face. 'Father's special legacy? Did you bring it?' She glanced at her sister. 'But isn't it rather . . . severe?'

Her sister shook her head. 'Don't be so silly, Nancy. It's an antique. And completely inappropriate. I don't believe the Wormling is even here. He must be on his assignment.' Her brow furrowed. 'A day earlier than arranged. No matter, Plan B is already operational.'

The smile dropped from her sister's lips. 'Plan B is dreadfully cruel, Agnes . . .'

Her sister slipped the knife back into the folds of her dress and nodded. 'Yes. I'm afraid it is.'

There was something about the look in her eyes that made Zorro feel very uncomfortable indeed.

PLAN B

Of the two children hiding in the park, only one of them was dead. The circumstances that had led Jake, a living boy, to be squatting behind a neatly trimmed privet hedge with Cora Sanderford, the ghost of a long-dead schoolgirl, were complicated to say the least, but it's enough to know that they shared an unlikely friendship of the sort that could only arise from them having saved the world together – not once, but twice. They weren't saving the world now, though. They were on an assignment. An assignment from the Embassy of the Dead.

'Remind me again why we can't do this tomorrow morning, like the Embassy asked?' whispered Cora. 'It's most unlike you to break protocol. You're normally such a stickler for the rules.'

Jake ignored her. This evening he was staying at his mum's house. Creeping out of *there* without her noticing was a different matter entirely. Besides, she had more choice of breakfast cereal than Dad.

He pulled his hoodie over his head and pulled the drawstrings tight so just his nose could be seen. It was cold and a bit damp – his least favourite type of weather. Jake looked at his phone. It was six a.m. and the sun was beginning to poke from behind the trees that fringed the edge of the park. It was the same hedge that he had climbed through to get into the park. He had the thin scratches on the backs of his forearms to show for it. Soon a park keeper would unlock the high gates and the park would fill with dog-walkers and children cutting through the grounds on their way to school. For now, the grounds were empty, and a thin mist drifted across the ruins of an ancient priory that had once dominated the surrounding villages but now served mainly as a location for dogs to urinate.

Despite the reluctance of all concerned, and because of his ability to see ghosts, Jake had been given the dubious honour of becoming the Embassy of the Dead's youngest *Undoer*: a member of the living enlisted to help ghosts trapped on the Earthly Plane to pass on to the Afterworld. His friend Cora was his assistant but he didn't call her that. Not to her face anyway.

It was the sort of job that meant he had to sneak out of his dad's house at four a.m. and cycle from his village to the next, to Undo a ghost. His dad would start work at five a.m. and when he poked his head around the door of Jake's room – like he always did – it would still be dark. Jake had stuffed the bed with pillows in the rough shape of a sleeping child.

He turned a file over in his hands and illuminated the words in the soft glow of his phone screen.

Digby Minter, bird-watcher b.1940 – d.1981

Type: medium-level poltergeist

He looked across at Cora, then back down at the file.

Recent reports in the local press of twigs being thrown at dog-walkers have been confirmed by this auditor as supernatural activity.

Twigs! It was hardly the most terrifying of ghostly activity. That reassured Jake immensely. Despite his unlikely career direction, he was highly averse to danger. He read on.

The nearest audited ghost is recorded as being Digby Minter, a medium-level poltergeist who has been waiting to be Undone since 1981. Because of this new activity – and its effect on the living – it has been decided to upgrade his status to Urgent.

Cause of Death: accidently crushed in the jaws of an earth mover whilst protesting against the building of the Hurlingford Bypass.

Then there was a signature:

Emerson Penceford, Ghost Auditor, the Embassy of the Dead

Cora tutted. 'A road which we now know never got built anyway.'

Jake nodded. They'd done their research. Every spirit trapped on the Earthly Plane had a reason for their predicament – one usually caused by some kind of trauma surrounding their death. Digby Minter's had been traumatic to say the least.

Jake glanced again at Cora. Her eyes were eagerly scanning the misty lawns. Like all ghosts, Cora had a reason for not having passed to the Afterworld.

She'd had such high expectations of her adult life that when she died young her spirit had lingered. Unlike most ghosts, though, Cora Sanderford didn't experience the 'longings' – an unfortunate emotional side effect of being stuck on the Earthly Plane. A wise old ghost had explained the feeling to Jake once.

'It's like there's a thread from your heart all the way to the Afterworld, and all those that you loved that died and didn't get stuck are tugging on it, trying to get you where you belong . . . with them.'

He smiled at the memory of his friend Stiffkey's Undoing. It had been Jake's first one. He could still picture the look of happiness that had passed across Stiffkey's face before he had disappeared into the Afterworld.

Cora glanced over at him. 'Why are you smiling like a weirdo, Precious?'

Jake pretended to ignore the nickname she'd given him when they'd first met. He'd fainted at the sight of what he thought was his own blood. Cora never let him forget that it had actually been ketchup. He cleared his throat. 'Digby Minter is still haunting the Earthly Plane because he thinks he died for

10

nothing. So if we let him know that the motorway never actually got built . . .'

Cora finished the sentence. 'He'll pass on to the Afterworld – in short, he'll be Undone!'

They high-fived and Jake felt a familiar chill as his hand passed soundlessly through hers. He touched his hoodie, feeling for his pendant necklace – a large tooth hanging from a leather thread – a memento of a brief trip into the Afterworld. He had found it in the branches of the Hangman's tree, sunk deep within the still waters of the Eternal Void.

Its presence was enough to fill him with a certain confidence.

'And that will be our third successful Undoing. We've the most out of any of the new Undoers, I think.'

Cora scratched the tip of her nose. 'Lucky you've got me helping you. Sanderfords *always* excel in their chosen field . . . That's what my father used to say.' She looked down at her hockey stick. 'I guess it's just a matter of agreeing what your chosen field should be.'

She swung her hockey stick at a weed and watched with satisfaction as the head was severed from the roots, flying over the lawns and sticking in the ruined masonry of the priory.

'He would have liked it here. Always wanted me to follow in his footsteps and study history.' She rolled her eyes. 'But who wants to live in the past when there's a present to explore?'

She laughed but to Jake it didn't sound like she'd convinced herself. He thought of the time when his mum and dad had split up. That was the past. They were both happy now, living their separate, slightly overlapping, grown-up lives. But it had taken Jake a while to get used to it. In a mixed-up, messed-up way, it had been him coming to terms with his own history that let him exist in the present at all.

He tried to think how to explain in a way that Cora might appreciate. But he couldn't fix it in his head. Instead he just nodded. He'd learnt it was easiest to just agree with Cora even if his compliance did sometimes lead him into danger.

'It does seem strange Digby's haunting here, doesn't it? Hurlingford must be thirty miles away.'

Cora shrugged. 'Maybe he's started to roam a little bit. Because of the long wait to be Undone.'

Jake scratched his head. 'Is that a thing?' He reached for his rucksack and took out a book titled *The Book of the Dead*. It was a guide to the dead, and more. He'd been presented with a copy at the ceremony when he'd officially become an Undoer.

Cora suddenly tensed and her hockey stick materialised in her hand. Her eyes lit up with excitement. 'Look!'

In the distance – about one hundred metres from where they hid – a large, robed figure shuffled across the lawns, his hunched form flickering between transparency and solidity.

'It's Digby Minter!' She looked at Jake and smiled. 'I'll wait with Sab.'

Sab was Jake's best friend. Sab had used to be insensitive to the presence of ghosts – in fact, Sab was pretty insensitive in general – but recently he'd started to show signs of being able to see some things, things that the average person couldn't. On the train back from their last adventure he'd seen Cora for the first time. There had been a lot of explaining to do, and the Embassy of the Dead had been informed. At the moment Sab was outside the park guarding his and Jake's bikes.

'Time to do your stuff, Wormling!' Cora called as she walked away.

Jake pulled a face at the slightly embarrassing codename the Embassy of the Dead had given him. He put the book carefully back in his rucksack and slung the bag over his shoulder, watching Cora slink away. Only a member of the living could Undo a ghost. The mere presence of Cora nearby would make it harder for that process to happen – something to do with the spectral energies of the two ghosts interfering.

Jake stood up and started walking towards the man. It was funny. No matter how many encounters he'd had with ghosts, Jake still felt on edge when he first met one. This time was no different.

He called out. 'Excuse me . . . Mr Minter?' Jake didn't want to startle him.

The hooded form stopped suddenly and looked sharply towards him.

Jake blinked.

There was something strange about the figure. *Why would a bird-watcher be wearing robes?*

14

Jake cleared his throat. 'I have some news for you. It's about the Hurlingford Bypass.'

The figure groaned, turned and started shambling, zombie-like, towards him.

Something was wrong. Something was very wrong.

'Jake? Jake? Are you there?' A tiny voice was calling out his name. At first Jake thought he'd pocket-dialled his mum somehow. Then he realised the sound was coming from his rucksack, not the pocket where he kept his phone. 'Jake?'

He took his rucksack off and knelt to rummage in it. The ghostly figure was shuffling slowly nearer.

Jake retrieved an intricately carved box from his rucksack. It was his Necrommunicator – a direct line to Wilkinson, his handler at the Embassy of the Dead. It was Wilkinson who had assigned him the Digby Minter case. Jake pushed the drawer open slightly and involuntarily shuddered at the sight of the dead mouse. Its shrivelled remains would channel Wilkinson's voice and actions for the duration of the call.

'I'm in the middle of something . . .' whispered Jake, looking nervously at the robed figure as it came nearer still. Digby Minter was a very large, imposing figure – that was the sort of information Jake would have liked to have seen on the file. So he could have prepared himself.

'Ah, the Minter case,' said Wilkinson through the mouse. 'Our second case together, and I'm very pleased that you've still not been lost. I'm pleasantly surprised.'

Jake blinked. 'Lost' was the word Wilkinson used instead of 'killed' – something which seemed to be one of the more unfortunate side effects of the job.

Jake watched the large ghost nervously. Each stumbling step brought the robed, hunched figure closer. 'Yes. The Minter case, I'm just about to Undo Digby Minter,' he said. 'At least I think I am—'

'About that, actually. . .' interrupted the mouse. Its little nose twitched – an echo of what Wilkinson was doing, far away at the Embassy of the Dead. 'Where is that stapler?' it muttered to itself.

The ghost was now only twenty metres away, and Jake could see him clearly. He was clad in rough brown robes, which were tied at the waist with rope.

A pale fleshy face hung low between giant shoulders, sandalled feet leaving no trace on the dewy ground. Jake squinted at a grainy passport photograph of Digby Minter that was paperclipped to the top of the file.

There wasn't much resemblance.

The mouse had fallen silent.

Jake sighed impatiently. 'Is it urgent?'

The mouse nodded. 'Very urgent. I just need to make sure this pile of papers is correctly stapled . . .'

There was another long pause.

'And?' Jake spluttered.

'Ah, here it is! Yes. What were we talking about, again? Oh, yes. Mr Minter. Turns out he was already Undone. A filing error by my predecessor, I'm afraid.'

Jake looked up as the ghost, just ten metres away, let out a low groan.

'So who is *this* ghost?'

'No idea,' came the reply. There was another short pause. 'Actually *some* idea . . . There is a small possibility it's the ghost of a monk, a Wandering Wight. The Embassy has been tracking him across Europe – last seen in France. Very dangerous. It seems he's on a never-ending pilgrimage of sites of religious interest. There's not one near you, is there?'

Jake looked around the ruins of the old monastery. 'Er . . . yes!'

The mouse continued. 'Well, if this chap you're seeing now *is* him, then don't let him know you're sensitive to his presence. He feeds on the energies of sensitive types like you. And get out of the grounds of whatever building he's visiting. The report says he can't leave sacred grounds until he is ready to move to the next place.'

Jake blinked as the mouse frowned. At least he thought it frowned. It was hard to tell on account of it being a mouse.

'We lost Badluck, an Undoer in our Paris division, at Notre Dame. A neat chap. Very well groomed. Apparently he didn't see the monk coming and . . .' The mouse fell silent again.

'*And what?*' Jake shook the box but the mouse lay still and unresponsive, as though Wilkinson's spirit had suddenly left the dehydrated rodent.

Jake blinked. Thirty seconds ago he had believed he was waving to the ghost of a bird-watcher to discuss the rerouting of the Hurlingford Bypass; now he realised he'd accidently hailed a Wandering Wight that wanted to feast on his soul.

Jake looked up. The monk had disappeared.

Get off the sacred ground.

He turned to run but it was too late. He felt strong arms wrap around his neck, choking him, pulling him downwards, enveloping him in the flapping robes of the monk. In the night air he smelt, for a second, a waft of sour wine and dust, as the Wandering Wight prepared to consume his soul . . .

DRAINING

It's hard to describe the feeling of your spirit energy being drained from your body. At first, when Jake felt the huge forearms of the Wandering Wight wrap tightly around his neck, it was a sudden electric jolt of panic. Though he could sense the strength of the monk, and feel the choking pressure of his arms, still, when he clawed at the Wight's wrists, Jakes fingers seemed to pass through them, like he was clawing at thin air. Then, as the energy flowed from his body to the monk's, the panic was replaced by a calm stillness and endless thoughts. Big thoughts about his mum and dad and their separate lives, thoughts about school, even trivial things like playing computer games. Then finally a feeling of tiredness, an inescapable fatigue - sleep creeping through his body - and for a moment he was curled up in the sleeping bag on the sofa bed, and his dad was poking his head around the door, the whispered words 'I love you' drifting into the distance, until there was just numbness broken only by a short, stabbing pain in his hand.

'I love you too, Dad,' he whispered, waking up.

He was back – back in the park, his fist clenched around the tooth that hung from his neck, feeling the pain of its sharp edges digging into his palm and a strange power flowing into his body. Jake was awake and struggling against the monk's vicelike grip, a rage taking hold of him now, refusing to let him give in. This time, his fingers seemed to reach through the thin air. The power of the tooth was allowing him to grasp the monk's arms, as though he was a living, breathing person. Jake's fingernails dug into soft flesh, and the monk grunted in pain and surprise, loosening his hold. Jake dropped and twisted from the grip, and for a second they stood staring at one another . . . until Jake turned and ran, going as fast as he could, gasping for air, stumbling across the lawns of the ruined priory.

He looked back over his shoulder. The monk was

following him, loping across the grass with surprising speed. He tried to take a short cut over a low section of ruined wall but he tripped, his legs refusing to move as he wanted, and he fell, the sharp flint edges ripping through his trousers. Then he was back on his feet, running towards some park gates.

Get off the sacred ground.

He reached the park gates. They were closed. Cora was nowhere to be seen but Sab was sitting, guarding the bicycles.

'What's up, Idiot?' he asked, looking up from his phone.

Jake was gasping for breath. He put his foot on the high gate and began to climb. 'Wrong ghost!' he managed to splutter. 'Soul-sucking Wight!'

Sab peered through the iron gates. 'I can't see anything . . .'

Jake quickly turned his head. The monk was lumbering ever closer. He looked angry. Jake grabbed one of the metal spikes and pulled himself higher.

'He can't leave the grounds of the abbey. I've got to get out.'

Sab scratched his nose. 'So we're going? Good, I

need something to eat before school starts – I'm starving.'

Jake straddled the top of the gate, carefully avoiding a spike. And just in time. The monk had reached the boundary. He reached for Jake's leg, his fingers clutching at Jake's shoe. Jake yanked it free from his grasp, tumbling over the top of the gate and falling to the ground outside the park.

From an aching pile on the ground he looked at the Wight on the other side of the gate. Their eyes locked and for a second Jake felt sorry for the ghost. Who knew what trauma had sentenced him to a death-time as a Wandering Wight?

'Can you really not see anything?' he asked Sab, not taking his eyes from the monk.

Sab squinted. 'Something. A shimmering perhaps. I think I'm getting better at this.' He beamed proudly.

Jake stood up and brushed the dirt from his school trousers, watching as the Wight stepped backwards from the gate and slowly disappeared to nothing. He sighed. 'That was too close. When I saw that the gate was locked I thought I was a goner!'

'Locked?' asked Sab. He reached forward and

turned the handle, swinging the gate open. 'It's open. I realised just after you'd squeezed through the hedge earlier.'

Jake glared. 'Why didn't you tell me?'

Sab shrugged again and got on his bike. 'I wondered why you were trying to climb over it.'

Jake looked around. 'Where's Cora?'

'Just coming,' said a voice. Cora was standing behind an information board that was positioned away from the gated entrance. 'I was reading up about the ruined priory . . .' She pulled a face at Sab. 'Can you see me, Idiot?' she asked, adopting Sab's nickname for Jake.

Sab smiled. 'I can a bit. You're wearing a weird straw hat.'

Cora ignored Sab's comment about her boater, and turned to Jake. 'Did you Undo Digby then, Precious?'

Jake shook his head. 'Not exactly. An angry monk almost killed me.'

She rolled her eyes. 'Any excuse.'

But Jake didn't notice. He was taking his phone out of his pocket. A message had arrived.

> Just checking you're up and
> ready for school, Dad x

His dad always signed his text messages like he'd never used a phone before. Jake tapped away on his own phone.

> Yup x

It wasn't a lie. He *was* up. And he was as ready for school as he would ever be.

THE MISSION
(7.45 A.M.)

The barber's on the high street had closed down. It wasn't the sort of thing Jake would normally notice, especially after the morning he'd had, but it seemed to have happened over the weekend. Now a white van was parked outside and a grey-haired man was heaving boxes of books from the back on to the pavement, and to be honest it was the most exciting thing that was happening in the high street at that particular moment – which wasn't saying much at 7.35 a.m.

The mission to the park had been planned by Cora with military precision to allow the boys enough time to cycle the six miles to the small town where Jake and Sab went to school afterwards. Unfortunately the unexpected presence of a Wandering Wight and Jake's hasty exit meant they now had to kill an hour before the school gates even opened.

They were sitting with their bikes on the high street, waiting for the café to open. Cora had spent the cycle ride possessing her old school trophy, which was safely tucked into Jake's rucksack. This was a side effect of her haunting – she was bound to a silver trophy Jake had taken from her old school's display cabinet. When the lid was open she was out; when the lid was closed she was stuck inside. Even when she was out, she couldn't venture more than thirty or so metres from the trophy, so Jake had to carry it everywhere.

'You're a bit like a genie!' Sab had joked when Jake and Cora had first explained this to him. 'Except without the three wishes!'

'That's a rubbish genie!' Jake had laughed until he saw Cora's glowering face. Cora would tease Jake mercilessly, and occasionally she didn't mind him teasing her back. Sometimes, though, Jake forgot that she really hated being confined to her trophy.

Freed from it now, Cora leant silently on her hockey stick, as Jake and Sab finished their packed

lunches approximately five hours before they were supposed to have started them – completing their daily ritual of switching one or two of their sandwiches to increase the variety. Sab's mum made him ham, cheese and iceberg lettuce. Jake, when he was at his dad's, made his own, usually cheese and pickle.

Together, the three children – two living, one dead – watched the grey-haired man lift a big box from the back of his car. He was the sort of person who could most politely be described as crumpled-looking. Beneath the mop of unruly grey hair was a lined and careworn face. He was wearing a tweedy jacket with suede elbow patches and a pair of faded green corduroy trousers ending above some battered brown leather shoes. A pair of reading glasses hung from his neck. The man put the box down and wiped the sweat from his brow with a sleeve. Then, groaning slightly with the exertion, he picked the box up again and disappeared into the old barbershop, a small unit, tucked between a permanently shuttered garage and the convenience store that only allowed two school children in at a time.

Cora wandered across the road. Even though she

was already dead – and if she was hit by a car it would simply pass straight through her – it didn't stop Jake wincing at the way she casually strolled across roads without looking. Also, he thought in annoyance, they had agreed that in public she would at least make some kind of effort to stay hidden. Just in case a passing member of the public happened to be sensitive to the presence of ghosts. It was simpler that way, but difficult to get Cora to actually agree to stay inside her trophy or even just keep to the shadows. Of course, they could just have closed the trophy and she'd have been sucked back inside, whether she wanted to go or not. It was just that it was always better to get her permission . . . or deal with an incredibly angry ghost the next time they opened the trophy.

Naturally, Jake's technique for crossing the road was much more cautious. After carefully looking both ways and back again, he joined her browsing through a box of old books outside the shop, leaving Sab to enjoy his mini-chocolate Swiss roll in peace. ('We don't share everything, Jake. Some things – like mini chocolate swiss rolls – are sacred.')

'What kind of bookshop is it?' Jake asked Cora

through a mouthful of sandwich, though to be honest, he wasn't particularly interested.

Cora shrugged. 'A dusty one.' She paused. Her eyes narrowed. 'Although this book might be of interest to us.' She pointed to a faded blue book, the spine of which was facing upwards from the box. Jake scratched his head. It had no title.

She looked at him with that half smile she did. Jake was never sure if she was laughing *with* him or *at* him.

'Why are you smiling like that?'

She raised her eyebrows.

'What?' He laughed, looking at the book again. The laughter died on his lips as he saw what she could see. Where once the spine had been plain, now a symbol appeared, embossed in silver: a triple cross.

Jake groaned.

'The logo of the Embassy of the Dead.' A voice sounded from the inside of the shop. The man was standing just inside the doorway, a bundle of books tucked under one arm.

'Greetings, Wormling,' he said, using Jake's given Undoer name. 'We've been expecting you . . .'

THE DEMONOLOGIST

Considering that yesterday the bookshop had been a busy barber's, the strange man had made incredible progress. Jake gazed around in wonder at the old books that lined the walls. The shop looked like it had opened centuries ago and – in all that time – had seen approximately zero custom.

Cora looked at the man. 'Are you a ghost?' she asked bluntly.

The man frowned at her. 'No. Well, yes. For the purpose of my visits to the Earthly Plane . . .' The man fished into his jacket pocket and pulled out a grey handkerchief, some coins, a folded bus ticket and a dented business card. He passed the card to Cora, who glanced at it briefly. Then she passed it to Jake. It was similar to Jake's own Undoer card, glossy black writing on a matt black background. Jake turned it over in the light and read the words that were neatly printed across its surface.

Doctor of Demonology

Jake blinked. 'Doctor of Demonology? Now *that's* a job!' He flipped the card over and read the other side.

Colin Brown

To be honest, Jake had been expecting a cooler name. Still, the next line was interesting:

University of Deadhaven, the Afterworld

'Deadhaven?' Jake looked at Cora. They'd seen the city of Deadhaven once, its lights twinkling in the distance. It was the City of the Dead. 'You're from the Afterworld?'

The man nodded. 'I'm happy to say that I passed to the Afterworld seamlessly some fifty years ago, after a particularly mundane death that

I don't care to elaborate on, which definitely wasn't embarrassing.' He coughed, reached for a book and handed it to Cora.

It fell through her hands. She glared at him crossly. 'It's rude to assume that all ghosts have a physical presence just because you do.'

'Of course. My apologies . . .' he mumbled.

Jake knew that ghosts could take any form, from solid through to immaterial. There were even some rare spectres who could flit between the two states. Cora, though, could not do this. She had some solidity, but not much. It meant she could pass through walls, but also that she was rubbish at playing computer games because she couldn't hold the controller. Only her hockey stick had a truly solid physical presence and even in her intangible hands it became a formidable weapon.

The man bent down, picked the book up off the floor, and handed it to Jake. 'Take this. You should read it, Green.'

Jake's eyes opened wide. It looked like a very long read. 'Now?'

'Whenever,' said the man.

Jake wasn't sure he had time to read a book, what with school work, computer games and Undoing – even one gifted him by a ghost. 'What is it about?' he asked.

'In part, it is a family history . . .' Colin Brown replied. He paused. 'Of sorts.'

'Whose?' asked Jake.

'That's the point.' The demonologist smiled. 'Yours.' He leant over and took the book back from Jake, opening it at a bookmarked page. 'It tells the story of the rising of Fenris the Fallen Reaper . . . You know something of him, I believe?'

Jake's heart sank at the mention of the reaper who had once, long ago, tried to overthrow the Afterworld Authorities; a reaper who believed that demons were the rightful masters of the living and the dead.

'I found a severed finger containing his trapped spirit,' said Jake. 'As you do. And then we saved the universe from his followers. People who wanted to bring his spirit back to life . . . I mean death . . . I mean . . . you know what I mean.' He looked at Cora for help.

Cora sighed. 'You tell the story so badly, Precious.' She turned to the demonologist. 'Basically, we saved the world.'

The demonologist nodded and placed his spectacles on his nose. 'Indeed. Your story has been recorded. At first we at the University of Deadhaven, chroniclers of history and predictors of the future, thought a cruel twist of fate had entrusted the safety of all humans, living and dead, to the hands of mere children.' His eyes twinkled as he peered at both of them in turn over the top of his spectacles. 'But then something turned up . . .' He paused and smiled at Jake. 'Do you have it? Do you have the tooth?'

Jake swallowed. His hands reached up to his neck and he pulled on the cord that held the tooth he'd found on the submerged tree in the black waters of the Eternal Void.

The demonologist's face broke into a happy grin at the sight of the large tooth dangling from the cord. His voice dropped to a whisper. 'Fascinating . . . fascinating.' He looked Jake in the eyes. 'It must be the one . . . Surely . . . Can I touch it?'

The demonologist reached forward. As he did, his hand pulled out further from his sleeve and Jake could see a mark, a tattoo on the man's wrist. A jagged, lopsided M.

The demonologist followed Jake's gaze and pulled his arm back. 'Of course, if you'd rather I didn't touch it, I quite understand. These things can have sentimental value.' He smiled kindly.

Jake felt uncomfortable. He didn't know why. It was just a tooth. Well, a tooth rescued from the depths of the Eternal Void. 'Erm . . . no. I'd rather you didn't.' Jake shielded the tooth with his hand. He looked towards the door of the shop, wanting to leave. The place smelt of old books, and the dust was starting to irritate his throat. Outside he could see Sab still engrossed in his phone. He was like a beacon, signalling Jake back to the real world. The normal world. The safe world. A world where kids could just be kids.

Jake preferred that world.

The demonologist smiled again. 'Of course, of course, I understand.' He stroked his chin thoughtfully. 'We need to validate it, that is all . . .' He looked at Jake and his brow furrowed. 'We need to be sure.'

'Sure of *what*?'

The demonologist reached into his pocket and took out an eyeglass. Screwing it into his eye socket, he leant towards Jake once more. 'Hold it still . . .' he said quietly. 'Hold it still.'

For a few seconds they stayed like that. Jake standing, slightly awkwardly, with an old man peering at the tooth strung around his neck. Then finally, with a groan, the demonologist straightened. Jake tucked the tooth back beneath his hoodie as the old man turned and reached for another book, placing it in Jake's hands. 'Read this too.' He reached for another. 'And this.' The doctor was excited. Now he scampered around the shop, taking books from everywhere and stacking them in Jake's arms until Jake was forced to put them down in a heap on a table.

'What did you need to be sure of?' Jake repeated.

The doctor stopped and turned to face Jake and Cora. 'You know what happened to Fenris after his fall? When his spirit was in hiding in the Earthly Plane? He took the body of a living man – so when the man's life ended Fenris could pass back into the Afterworld undetected and restart what he'd begun.'

'But the Embassy of the Dead trapped his spirit in the composer's finger,' said Jake.

The demonologist nodded. 'But that is near history.' He scratched his head. 'What do you know of the time *before* Fenris was chased from the Afterworld?'

Jake shook his head. 'Not much.'

The demonologist took the first book back from Jake and leafed through its pages. 'Do you know of the demon army he raised? Do you know of the battle of Deadhaven? And have you heard of Uthred Dragon?' He held the book open at an old inked illustration. A Viking warrior stood on a rock, holding a huge axe and gazing out over a sea.

Cora was puzzled. 'I've heard of Uthred. I think. Can't quite remember where though.' She shrugged and looked at Jake. 'It's been a while since my history classes, to be fair.'

But Jake wasn't listening. 'Uthred Dragon!' he murmured. Now that *was* a cool name. 'But what does that have to do with—'

The demonologist held up his finger for silence, and began to read from the book.

'Uthred Dragon had spent his entire lifetime fighting. It was all he knew. From his boyhood in the small village in Daneland, through his teenage years earning his place as a Viking warrior chieftain, and on to adulthood. By the time he was thirty he had crossed the North Sea with an army of warriors, waged war across ancient Britain, and then crossed the Channel, where he died aged thirty and a day, taking a lucky arrow to the eye, while storming the beaches of France. He arrived in the Afterworld with three hundred of his warriors and the blood of thousands on his axe.'

The demonologist looked up from the book to make sure they were paying attention.

They were.

'If his men had sought a peaceful afterlife they would be disappointed. But for Uthred Dragon the timing was perfect. A war was raging between the Afterworld Authorities – a combination of ancient demon families and the dead – and a band of powerful rebel demons, led by Fenris, who fought to plunge the worlds of living and dead into chaos.'

Jake stared at the demonologist. 'You mean there were demons fighting for both sides?'

The demonologist nodded. 'Indeed.' His fingers traced the words in the book where he'd been interrupted.

'A great battle was waged on the outskirts of Deadhaven in the Afterworld. The dead fell in great numbers, their bodies disappearing to the ether, as they fell upon the demon weaponry. Only the greater demons known as reapers, still loyal to the Authorities, could even dream of facing Fenris in combat, for he was the strongest and most savage of them all. One of these reapers, Mawkins of the Hare, marched out with a phalanx of bonewulf to meet him.'

Jake shuddered. He remembered Mawkins – a demon built of the soil and of the trees, the grimmest of grim reapers, whose scythe could cut a hole to the Eternal Void, but who was – when all was said and done – a friend of the good and an enemy of the forces of Fenris.

'Mawkins and Fenris fought for two days, until eventually Mawkins fell, his shoulder clamped and torn in the jaws of Fenris, who was occupying his monstrous lupine form.'

'Monstrous lupine form?' Jake looked at Cora.

'It means wolf-like. A giant wolf,' Cora hissed. 'Stop interrupting!'

'The army of the Authorities watched with horror as Fenris prepared to administer the death blow to Mawkins – the strike that would surely mean the defeat of all that was great and good about the Afterworld; a strike that would mean the enslavement of all the living and the dead. But a lone figure stood forward from the crowd, and Fenris scoffed as he saw that it was a mere member of the dead. But this warrior was no normal deadman. This warrior was Uthred Dragon.'

'*Such* a cool name,' whispered Jake to himself. Cora rolled her eyes.

'Uthred swung his mighty axe as Fenris leapt, cleaving the wolf's bottom jaw in half. Seeing Fenris so injured, the armies of the Afterworld Authorities, humans and demons alike, rallied and drove the rebel demons from Deadhaven towards the Outerlands of the Afterworld.'

Cora swung her hockey stick through the air in the motion of one cleaving the jaw of a monstrous lupine demon. 'That's when Fenris fled to the Earthly Plane.'

Jake nodded glumly. 'And all my problems started.'

The demonologist cleared his throat, and continued reading.

'Uthred Dragon took one of Fenris' teeth from the broken jaw as a trophy. He marched with the Authorities' army until they faced the broken and demoralised demon army. Fenris had fled and the remaining rebel demons were driven into the Eternal Void.'

The demonologist paused and gazed at the tooth once more. 'Fenris could cross between the Eternal Void, the Earthly Plane and the Afterworld by tearing a hole in the air with his teeth. This lost tooth became the Authorities' greatest weapon, and with it, the rebel demons were sent to the Eternal Void.'

'One of the rebel demons could survive in the Eternal Void. Its name was the Hangman, so called for its habit of draping the remains of the dead in the branches of trees. Uthred spoke to his men: "Today my final battle will be fought, but tomorrow my heir will rise and he shall bear the tooth trophy of Uthred Dragon, the demon-slayer. The lineage of demon kings shall be ended for all time."'

The demonologist looked up from the book and read the last part from memory:

'Ignoring the wisdom of his celestial allies and the pleas of his men, Uthred Dragon waded into the Void to slay the final rebel demon. He was never seen again. The tooth was lost for ever.'

Jake's hand crept to his pendent. He swallowed nervously. 'You mean this is the tooth of Fenris?'

The demonologist closed the book and spoke to Jake. 'You know what the ancient Norse bards called the young of dragons in their tales and songs around the fireside?'

Jake shook his head. 'I literally have no idea.'

A voice sounded from behind them. 'They called them *wormlings*, Mr Green. Wormlings. *You* are the heir to Uthred Dragon, Jake. You are the chosen one.'

Jake's mouth dropped open. The quiet was eventually broken by Cora.

'God help us all,' she said.

THE GOMSEER

The voice had come through an open doorway. Jake and Cora turned towards the sound to see a figure sitting in a high-backed, studded leather armchair that was positioned in such a way that only a hand was visible.

Jake blinked. The room was much larger than could have ever fitted into the old barber's.

Cora gripped her hockey stick tightly and was about to step into the room when the demonologist held up a cautioning finger.

'It is an apparition,' he whispered. 'What you see and hear is a projection from the Afterworld . . .'

Cora paused and then addressed the seated figure. 'Who are you?' she demanded.

The speaker ignored her. 'I sensed it when we first met, Jake. I sensed you were *special*. Of course,

I could not have foreseen that you were the heir to Uthred Dragon. Not until I heard you had found a tooth in the Hangman's tree! But we needed to make sure. Hence the demonologist's presence.'

The demonologist bowed his head slightly. 'It is an honour to be of assistance.'

The other man stood up from the chair. The first thing that Jake noticed was that his head was not on his shoulders where you might expect it to be – instead, it was tucked neatly under his arm. Actually, it was the only thing that Jake noticed for a moment, before the man turned to face him and Jake's memory kicked in. 'Tokelo Fortune, the Minister of Security for the Afterworld!'

The man who had named him Wormling. The guest of honour at the ceremony where he had been given the position of Undoer.

Tokelo Fortune beamed. 'You remember me! How satisfying. When the name Wormling came to my lips I was as surprised as you were. I had no idea you'd turn out to have such a pedigree.' He burst into a short peal of laughter.

Jake nodded. How could he forget a man with a

removable head?

Minister Fortune chuckled and motioned around the room in which he stood. 'Splendid, isn't it? These are my private chambers in the Afterworld. Part of the perks of being a minister. I'd invite you through to have a look around if it wasn't just an illusion.'

Cora shrugged. 'It's OK. We had a very similar reading room at St Bodelean's School,' she said sulkily. 'A little bigger perhaps.'

Tokelo Fortune smiled warmly. 'It's interesting, Ms Sanderford. You are one of the only females to ever glimpse inside this room, for it has only been in the last two hundred years that women have even been allowed to hold the position of minister, and there has still yet to be a female Minister of Security.'

Cora shook her head in disgust.

The demonologist smiled. 'The Afterworld Authorities are slowly catching up with modern times. In the early days, though, it was very different.' He motioned to a shelf of ancient books. 'For example, one theory posits that early dead scholars of the Afterworld excised all mention of women from the original chronicles of Afterworld history, apportioning their triumphs to their male counterparts.'

'Typical,' said Cora with a sigh.

The demonologist huffed slightly. 'It's a very recent theory. I'd treat it with scepticism if I were you.'

Tokelo Fortune clicked his fingers, and a shape scuttled across the thick patterned carpet towards where he stood. Jake recoiled in horror at the sight of a huge spider-like creature – eight spindly legs holding an abdomen the size of a rugby ball with a small vicious-looking head wielding a pair of savage pincers. A thin, tube-like proboscis curled above its head.

Tokelo Fortune stooped and picked it up. 'Don't mind the Gomseer,' he said, stroking its shiny abdomen with a single finger. He pointed at the curled proboscis. 'Its bite can paralyse then desiccate the living or the dead, but once you have gained its trust it makes an admirable pet. One that must be treated with respect, mind.'

Jake looked at Cora. 'What's desiccate?'

She rolled her eyes. Again. 'It means to dehydrate.

So you become a dried-up husk.' She pulled a face at Tokelo Fortune. 'Funny sort of pet though.'

Tokelo chuckled. 'Indeed, but a useful one . . .'

He took a small package from a table beside him, and held it in front of the Gomseer. Jake watched in horror as its proboscis slowly uncurled to feel the package as it turned it around in its mandibles.

Tokelo placed the Gomseer on the rug. It scuttled away into the darkness, carrying the package. He smiled at Cora warmly. 'A delivery for someone special . . .'

Cora looked at Jake. 'Very romantic! Roses are red, violets are blue, here's a box of chocolates delivered by a giant spider that could turn you into a dehydrated husk . . .'

Jake scratched his head, trying to push the image of a dried-out, husk-like corpse to the back of his mind. 'I don't understand . . .' he said. 'How can I be the heir to a demon-slayer? How can I be the Chosen One? My mum's a nurse and my dad's a handyman.'

Tokelo smiled. 'The roots of the past take twisted turns. Who knows where or when a bud will finally break ground. I sensed it, when we met. We have been waiting for the heir's arrival for a long time . . . I had a vision, there and then on the stage of the Embassy of the Dead with you standing before me: a child in the shadow of a wolf, a tooth in their hand and . . .' He stopped himself midsentence. He shook his head and frowned. 'It was not clear . . . The child's face was obscured. I could not be sure until I heard about the tooth.' He reached into his pocket to retrieve a handkerchief and dabbed it against his mouth. 'It was *you*, Jake. It *had* to have been you. You have found the tooth. And the prophesy has begun to be fulfilled . . .' He smiled. 'Now is our time to strike.'

'Strike?' Jake swallowed hard. *Strike* sounded dangerous.

The demonologist rubbed his hands together. 'You really are the most wonderful discovery! It's big news.'

Tokelo raised a finger to silence him. 'It's big news, yes. But it's dangerous news too. That is why the Embassy of the Dead are being excluded from this meeting. I've taken the liberty of disabling their line of communication to you for multiple reasons. In fact, this mission and our true calling are only known between the four of us. For the sake of the living and the dead.'

Jake looked at Cora. 'That might explain the Mousephone not working.' He paused as he noticed the sulky expression on her face. 'Are you OK?'

She nodded, then forced a smile. 'I'm fine, Precious,' she said in a way that indicated she was anything but. 'Absolutely fine.'

Tokelo continued. 'Only we at the Ministry of Security know of the tooth's true origin. But this will just be a matter of time. It has great power. Someone will come for the tooth and they won't let a child stand in their way.'

'Two children,' said Cora.

Jake nodded, grateful for the support. The thought of the tooth being taken from him made his guts tighten.

'You *have* confirmed it is the tooth of the reaper Fenris?' Tokelo Fortune asked the demonologist.

The demonologist cleared his throat. 'It is Fenris' tooth.'

Tokelo smiled. 'You will of course have noticed it can sometimes be used to open a passage to the Void. A side effect of it having belonged to a reaper.'

Jake had used the tooth's powers once already, ripping a hole between the Earthly Plane and the Eternal Void. In the course of that incident the Void had sucked a particularly virulent plague demon to his demise.

Jake thought back to his meeting with Mawkins the reaper. Mawkins' scythe had worked the same way, cutting a passage to the Eternal Void as Fenris tore holes with his teeth. He nodded as Tokelo Fortune continued.

'The tooth might also enhance your powers. Have you noticed an increased sensitivity to spirits? Visions? Have those around you felt its powers change them?'

Jake swallowed. He wasn't too comfortable talking about this kind of thing. This morning in the ruins the tooth had given him the power to grip the arms of the Wandering Wight. It might also explain why Sab had started to be able to see Cora. Maybe it was affecting him too?

There was an awkward silence that was broken

by Cora. 'What do you mean by, "Now is our time to strike"?'

Tokelo Fortune placed his head on his shoulders and began to pace around his private chambers. 'After the Chosen One vanquished Malthus the plague demon from the Earthly Plane, the Embassy of the Dead uncovered a list of encrypted names in the Captain's quarters: all demons that were plotting the downfall of the Afterworld Authorities. The names were decoded and the Afterworld Authority forces struck quickly and ruthlessly. The plotters – all demons – were wiped out. All but one.'

Jake groaned. There was always one.

A frown darkened Tokelo Fortune's brow. 'The Afterworld is ruled by a council of the dead that represents those who once lived on the Earthly Plane, and a royal family of demons who represent the celestial creatures who originally inhabited the Afterworld. The king of demons is elderly, a benevolent creature who believes in the dead and demons living in peace alongside one another. But he has a son, a prince by the name of Arkus the Invincible. Spoilt, arrogant and insolent . . .' Tokelo took a step closer to the doorway. 'Arkus the Invincible was the last name on the decoded list. His father is old. His deathtime draws close. And when he dies, Arkus will inherit the demon throne.' He scowled deeper. 'A follower of Fenris would share control of the Afterworld Authorities!'

Cora looked at Jake. 'What happens when a demon dies? Where do they go?'

The demonologist smiled. 'Their essence joins the fabric of the Afterworld. All demons are from – and become – the world into which the living will eventually pass.'

Cora pulled a face. 'Of course. Makes perfect sense.'

Tokelo Fortune chuckled. 'If you'd let me continue, Ms Sanderford . . . The knowledge of Arkus's allegiance to Fenris is shared by but a few at the Ministry of Security. Arkus the Invincible currently hides in plain sight – posing as loyal to the Afterworld Authorities.'

Jake scratched his head. 'Hiding? So you want me to find him?'

'No, Jake.' Fortune stopped pacing and turned so

his disembodied spectral head, tucked beneath his arm once again, could look Jake full in the eye. 'Fenris' tooth has another property, for he was a reaper, and a reaper is the only being that is capable of sending a royal demon to the void. A reaper . . .' He looked at Jake, smiling. 'Or the tooth of a reaper.'

Jake's fingers crept nervously to his pendant as Tokelo Fortune continued.

'In short, Wormling, I don't want you to find him. I want you to kill him.'

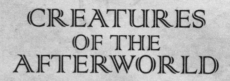

CREATURES OF THE AFTERWORLD

GOMSEER:

This giant deathmite — now usually referred to by its correct demon name of Gomseer — is a domesticated creature-demon. Originally farmed as pets for demon aristocracy, the keeping of deathmites now requires a strict licence from the Ministry of Security, due to their preference for feeding on spirit energy.

The Gomseer has been known to grow up to 50 cms in diameter, and can be distinguished

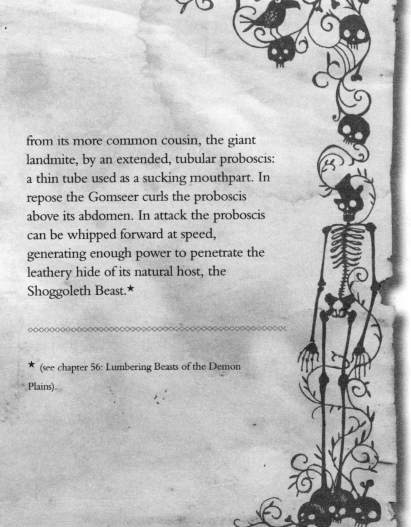

from its more common cousin, the giant landmite, by an extended, tubular proboscis: a thin tube used as a sucking mouthpart. In repose the Gomseer curls the proboscis above its abdomen. In attack the proboscis can be whipped forward at speed, generating enough power to penetrate the leathery hide of its natural host, the Shoggoleth Beast.★

⬦⬦⬦

★ (see chapter 56: Lumbering Beasts of the Demon Plains).

BUBBLE WRAP

'What's up with you, Jake? Been staying up playing computer games all night?'

Jake blinked awake from his daydream. The voice came from his maths teacher, Ms Pike, who, on the scale of teachers, rated somewhere between quite nice and lovely. She smiled at him and he felt himself blushing.

'No, Miss,' he muttered and he started writing down random numbers from the weird triangle diagram on the whiteboard.

He wished he had been up all night playing computer games, like a normal kid. He looked around the classroom, its grubby school carpet and joyless walls filling him with a sense of comforting normality.

Ms Pike smiled. 'Remember an isosceles triangle has two equal sides and two equal angles.'

Jake squinted at the paper. She might as well have been talking in a foreign language. He hadn't listened to a word she'd said since he'd sat down.

Understandably, considering just that morning he'd been told he was the Chosen One, aka the demon-slayer.

He looked over to Sab who was watching him slyly. Sab made a heart shape with his fingers. Jake rolled his eyes and stared at his worksheet again. You'd think being the Chosen One would make it unnecessary to learn pointless geometry. But it seemed not . . .

At lunchtime, Jake and Sab discussed the morning's happenings over a packet of crisps they'd combined all their loose change to buy, after remembering at lunchtime they'd already eaten their packed lunches.

'You're the Chosen One?' Sab *had* said, tipping out the remnants of the bag of bacon-flavoured crisps into his open mouth. 'It's got a nice ring to it but . . .'

He paused, suppressing a smile. 'The Chosen *Idiot* sounds more accurate!'

He laughed, spraying crisp crumbs down his front.

Jake rubbed the back of his head. 'That joke doesn't even work.' To be fair, though, the thought of anybody choosing him for anything did seem unlikely. Chosen by whom? And didn't he even get a say in the matter?

He thought back to Cora's reaction to the news. Usually she was excited by the prospect of danger, especially if it involved going on some kind of adventure. But this time . . . this time she'd seemed annoyed.

He sighed. She was probably a bit jealous. After all, wasn't the fact that she felt she hadn't had the chance to live up to her expectations the reason she'd become a ghost? If she couldn't experience life to the full . . . *She certainly seemed dedicated to experiencing death to the full instead.*

Thinking about it, she *had* seemed annoyed by Jake being the Chosen One, rather than her, which to be honest was totally unfair. He didn't even want to be the Chosen One!

Jake scratched his head. Girls, especially spectral girls, were very confusing.

After school, Sab came back to Jake's mum's house. The bus dropped them off by the pub and they walked a little way before opening the trophy and releasing Cora. Jake dawdled behind while Cora and Sab walked ahead, discussing everything that had happened. Being in the village, walking past the same old places, smelling the same old smells, made Jake feel better. With each step the thought of it being him who had to assassinate an invincible demon seemed less and less likely.

There's been a misunderstanding, somewhere. Of course it's a misunderstanding . . .

By the time he got to his mum's house he'd convinced himself that this rather awkward situation would blow over. Cora and Sab were waiting for him at the door with Zorro.

'Clever Zorro . . . You always know where we're going to be, don't you?' Jake was positively cheery now. He smiled at Cora. 'Surprised you didn't just float through the door.'

She laughed. 'That would've been awfully rude!'

Sab lifted up a welly boot on the small porch, picked up a key, and unlocked the front door. 'Has your mum bought any snacks yet?' he asked, walking in.

Mum was out, and there were no snacks. Instead, a small parcel was waiting for Jake on the table. His heart dropped. He sat down with his head in his hands. 'I hate mystery boxes. They always seem to contain something dead or severed.'

Sab scratched his head. 'Maybe it's something run-of-the-mill. Like a present from Auntie Hilda.'

Jake hung his coat over the back of the chair. 'That would only be run-of-the-mill if I had an Auntie Hilda, which I don't.' He frowned and pointed at the top of the package. 'Can you see it, Sab?'

A strange symbol was beginning to form beneath the address.

'See what?' said Sab. He sighed. 'Don't forget I'm not as sensitive as you . . .' His eyes suddenly widened. 'Wait! I *do* see it. Just faintly. It's like a weird triple cross . . . That's the logo, right?'

Jake nodded. 'It's the emblem of the Embassy of the Dead.' A thought dawned on him and he looked up at Cora. 'At least it can't be from Tokelo Fortune. He said the Embassy must be kept in the dark about me having to . . .' He couldn't bring himself to say it. Instead he picked the package up. It was about a foot in diameter and wrapped in brown paper.

'You should open it,' said Sab, sending food spraying from his mouth. He was now standing behind Jake, with his arm up to the elbow in a packet of cereal.

Cora grimaced. 'Despite his appalling table manners, I'm afraid I have to agree with Sab. Last time we ignored the Embassy of the Dead you ended up wrestling with a mad old lady underneath a table in the shed.' She smiled affectionately at the thought of one of the previous times they'd saved the Earthly Plane.

Jake lowered his head to the table, his voice emerging muffled. 'I just think it's best to not open it. Like the famous saying goes: "No problem is too big to not ignore."'

Cora frowned. 'That's not a famous saying. I'm not sure it's a saying at all.'

Jake opened his rucksack and took out the

Necrommunicator. He turned it around in his hands. 'If only we could ask Wilkinson.'

'Are you sure it's broken?' asked Cora.

Jake pushed the drawer open and peered in. Everything looked the same inside. It was hard to imagine how a dehydrated mouse corpse could look any worse, though.

Cora stared at it. 'That's the problem with this kind of thing. It's hard to know how to fix it.'

Jake nodded.

Sab grinned. 'Maybe it needs a software update?'

Jake ignored him. 'We should take advice from somewhere. We can't just open the box! Who knows what curse we might—'

'Ooh, bubble wrap!' said Sab. They looked round to see him beaming proudly and holding up the open box in one hand and a bundle of bubble wrap in the other.

Cora laughed. 'Well, that's solved that problem, then.'

Sab's eyes suddenly widened. He swore as something fell from the bottom of the bubble wrap, a delicate glass thing, tumbling through the air.

'No!' Jake shouted, lurching from his chair and diving forward. In that split second, the myriad of punishments for Sab breaking something that the Embassy of the Dead had sent them flashed through his mind. Imprisonment . . . Mawkins the reaper . . . Being thrown into the Eternal Void . . .

His fingers grabbed at the glass thing, and for a moment it seemed safe, but then, as his body impacted with the floor, it slipped from his grasp, spinning up into the air and then spiralling downwards, towards the hard stone tiles.

He was too far away now. He closed his eyes to protect them from the inevitable explosion of glass.

But it didn't come.

He reopened his eyes and saw the object – a delicate cocktail glass – hovering just six inches from the ground. He blinked. The glass appeared to be full of a sparkling liquid.

Sab's jaw dropped open. 'Oh. My. Days!'

Then the glass slowly began to rise again, higher and higher from the floor. Jake watched as it stopped ascending through the air and hovered in front of his eyes. A hand was starting to form around the stem, then a forearm appeared, and a shoulder, and then suddenly the whole body: an elegantly suited young man, with an unfastened bow tie swinging from a slender neck.

'Eustace Carmichael-Bancombe,' breathed Jake, with considerable relief. He was an old friend, the cloakroom attendant at the Embassy of the Dead.

Sab stared between everybody, then back to Eustace, still popping the bubble wrap absentmindedly. 'That was some entrance!'

The corner of Eustace's mouth crept into a slight smile. 'One should always make an effort . . .' He gazed around at the three children. 'However dull the party appears!' He bowed dramatically. 'Eustace Carmichael-Bancombe at your service.' He looked at Sab and Cora then down at Jake, who was still sprawled across the floor. 'Consider this a summons from the Embassy of the Dead.'

The room fell into silence.

Sab popped another bubble. 'Am I coming, then?'

Eustace rolled his eyes. 'Yes.' He grimaced at Zorro. 'And the fox too, unfortunately.'

'Cool, cool . . .' muttered Sab, reluctantly putting

down the bubble wrap, but not before one last frantic squeeze. He looked up at Eustace. 'Is it difficult? Travelling to the Embassy, I mean.'

Eustace smiled and took a sip from his cocktail. 'Not at all. Not at all. You just have to die a little.'

DYING A LITTLE

By now Jake was familiar with the process of being summoned to the Embassy of the Dead. *Leave your life at the door.* That was the policy. Easy enough if you were already dead like Zorro or Cora, but for Jake and Sab it meant their spirits leaving their bodies.

Eustace could help with that. He was a ghost blessed with the rare talent of bodyshifting: the ability to separate a spirit from its living body. Once outside of their bodies, the Embassy simply needed to summon them. The Embassy of the Dead had their own Summoning Wight to perform that very task, a ghost by the name of Herman Poltago, friendly enough but, like the Wandering Wight in the ruined priory, with a nasty habit of trying to drain the spirit energy from any being around him.

Last time Jake had been summoned by a Wight he'd had the former champion Undoer, Bad Penny, to help him leave his body. This time however it was the turn of Eustace. It was time for a bodyshift!

Eustace placed his hand on Jake's shoulder. 'Now step backwards, Jake, old chap.'

Jake took a deep breath, then a pace backwards. Before him his body stood limply with Eustace's hand still on its shoulder. Jake shuddered. He would never get used to the sensation of seeing his soulless body – his meat suit, as Eustace would say – standing numbly before him.

From the chair in the corner of the kitchen, Sab looked up from his phone, his eyes flicking between Jake's ghost and Jake's body. 'You're . . . you're . . . you're . . .' His mouth didn't seem to be working properly.

Eustace perched on the arm of the chair and now placed a comforting hand on Sab's shoulder. 'Discombobulating, isn't it? The first time you see it, I mean.'

Sab jumped up and away from Eustace. 'There's no way you're doing that to me.'

Eustace chuckled. 'Oh, but I already have.'

Sab spun round and saw Eustace still with his arm on Sab's own vacant body's shoulders. His body was sitting on the chair, head slumped forward, his phone gripped in his lifeless hands. Sab stared down at his ghost legs. 'I'm see-through!' he declared in horror.

Eustace toasted Sab with his cocktail glass. Then he looked down at Zorro, frowning. 'The fox is a bit tricky. To get him back here I need some kind of spectral tether.' He pointed to Sab and Jake's limp bodies. 'You living ones can be recalled from your bodies. Bad Penny's "special technique", I believe it's called.'

'Basically splashing our bodies with freezing water,' explained Jake to Sab.

Eustace looked at Jake's rucksack, sitting unzipped on the floor. 'Cora can be retrieved by closing her trophy, thus forcing her to return to her possessed item.' He frowned again. 'But what to use for Zorro? We need something personal to him. Something that we can hold on to to get him back.'

Cora looked at Jake. 'What about Jake himself? Zorro follows him everywhere.'

Eustace raised his glass to Jake. 'Yes! Jake would be perfect.' His eyes twinkled. 'It might be a tiny bit traumatic for you, I'm afraid, but it's a way Zorro can be brought back from the Embassy.'

Jake blinked.

Traumatic?

'What does it involve?' he asked, his eyes narrowing.

'Just some old magic. I'll clear its use with the Embassy, of course.'

Eustace glanced into his cocktail glass and added quickly: 'We would need to make a herb poultice using not a small amount of your blood.'

'Gross,' said Sab.

Jake shook his head in disbelief. 'Surely there's another way, Eustace?'

Eustace shrugged. 'Well, nowadays some prefer to use animal meat instead of the blood poultice. Do you have any?'

'Animal meat? There's a packet of ham in the fridge,' said Jake hopefully. 'Will that do?'

'Half a packet actually,' added Sab guiltily. 'I ate some.'

Eustace nodded. 'That will be perfect. It's actually more effective than human blood and slightly more ethical too, being that the pig is already dead and its spirit is already safely in the Afterworld.'

Sab looked a bit sick.

Jake held his hands out in exasperation. 'To be honest, next time you do this I'd suggest trying that way first, Eustace.'

Eustace shrugged. 'It lacks panache. Are you sure you'd rather proceed with the ham-based method to bring Zorro back?'

'Yes.'

Eustace bowed slightly. 'As you wish.'

His eyes flicked up to the clock on the wall. 'Goodness, it's time for the summon—'

Before he could finish, Jake felt himself sinking into darkness, and the light shrank away until all he could see was a tiny pinprick in the far distance.

Somewhere far away, in the ruined country house that was the base for the Embassy of the Dead, he knew he was being called.

The pinprick of light began to grow again – slowly at first, then larger and larger, and Jake knew that his spirit was almost at its destination. Despite the strange feeling of floating through the ether, despite the secret mission he'd been set by the Afterworld Authorities, and despite the summons from his superiors at the Embassy of the Dead, something else popped into his head. Something that filled his heart with cold dread.

His mum was due home in an hour . . .

He'd completely forgotten! What would happen when his mum came in and found his and Sab's bodies sitting unresponsive round the kitchen table?

'We are in so much trouble,' he said to himself, blinking in the bright light that flooded his brain.

'Welcome to the Embassy of the Dead, dude,' replied a voice.

HERMAN POLTAGO

Jake squinted in the light. He was sitting in an uncomfortable plastic chair, at a little table, in a small windowless room. The table was divided by a thick glass partition that spanned the entire width of the room. On the other side of the table, behind the glass, sat the man who had spoken.

'Hey, Jakey! Long time, no see, my man!'

'Hello, Herman,' said Jake, smiling as he recognised the Summoning Wight of the Embassy of the Dead. Despite Herman Poltago being a Wight – who, if the glass partition was removed, wouldn't be able to resist sucking the spectral energy from Jake's body until Jake had disappeared from all existence – Jake quite liked him.

Maybe it was his smiley, slightly teasing eyes that reminded Jake a bit of his dad. Tall and scruffy, with a smile always lurking beneath the surface ready to pop out at any moment, Herman Poltago had a straggly beard and a sunken, sunburnt face. Jake started as the Wight doubled over suddenly and began coughing. Jake waited. He knew that Herman Poltago's life had ended falling off a yacht – his ghost was trapped on the Earthly Plane by the irony of him having slipped on a literal banana skin – and one of the side effects of his haunting was the unfortunate habit of occasionally regurgitating seaweed and other seaborne detritus. Herman disappeared behind the table for a bit then appeared again holding a small fish.

'Don't see that every day!' he said, dropping the minnow into a wastepaper bin. He wiped his hands on his Hawaiian shirt and took a piece of paper from his drawer, sliding it through a small slot in the glass. He rolled his eyes. 'You know how the Embassy loves paperwork.'

Jake picked up a pen that was attached to the table with coiled wire. He signed his name twice because the first time the pen ran out of ink and needed shaking. He slid the form back through the slot, and Herman looked at it, then handed Jake a ticket numbered 312.

Jake glanced at the ticket. The number would keep changing – counting down the time he had left in the Embassy of the Dead before his spirit would be unable to rejoin his body.

Herman added the signed papers to a large messy pile, and took off his sun hat to reveal a bald patch in the middle of his long, straggly hair. 'It's busy today. Lots of coming and going, so you've not got long.'

Jake looked at his ticket dubiously as the number ticked down to 311. Eustace had said something about the Ambassador having a reception. He shuddered at the thought of meeting the Ambassador. You'd think what with having saved the Earthly Plane and the Afterworld twice she'd give him a break. No chance.

Herman nodded to the ticket in Jake's hand. 'Your handler – whatshisname – will contact Eustace when your number starts to get to single digits.'

As always, it would be up to someone else to bring him back – in this case, Eustace. Jake hoped Eustace wouldn't get distracted.

He looked at the ticket one last time and then put it back in his pocket just as the door to the room opened and a neatly dressed man walked in. Jake recognised his handler Wilkinson. He was holding a plate of sausage rolls and smiling proudly.

'My! That was very quick, Jake. This time you arrived faster than Cora and the fox. Very surprising. Usually people who have been out of their bodies longer arrive first. Your sensitivity to these things must be increasing.'

Jake shrugged, but his hand instinctively went up to where his tooth pendant was hanging from his neck beneath his hoodie. Hadn't Tokelo Fortune said the tooth might enhance his powers?

He smiled as he felt the reassuring bump beneath his clothes. One of the properties of spectral objects, like the tooth or the Mousephone, was that they would travel with the spirit, and not leave a physical object behind in their place. Unlike, say, a pair of trousers, that both travelled with the spirit and left a physical form behind with the body.

Jake resisted looking at the rangy and straggle-bearded Herman.

It was lucky about the trousers, otherwise all ghosts would be naked.

Herman Poltago waved him away from the chair. Cora was materialising and Jake smiled even more broadly, as the cross look on her face upon realising he had got there first was replaced by her own smile at the discovery that she was solid.

Wilkinson proffered a sausage roll which was gratefully received by Cora, who shoved it into her mouth whole and reached out for another.

Jake scratched his head. 'And you say Sab's table manners are bad.'

'Sab eats all day, every day. I only get to eat here,' she said with flaky pastry crumbs all round her mouth.

Zorro was next to arrive. Then finally, after a minute, Sab materialised on the chair. He was fast asleep. Jake woke him and introduced him to everyone. Like Jake, Sab had to sign a piece of paper and was issued with a ticket. The number was 200 – far lower than Jake's.

'What does this mean?' asked Sab.

'It means that you'll die before me if something goes wrong,' said Jake.

Sab looked at him blankly.

'Also, I forgot to mention to Eustace that my mum will be home in an hour. If we're not back in time she's liable to find our two lifeless bodies sitting upright around the kitchen table. She is not going to be pleased.'

A look of terror crossed Sab's face. 'We'd better a get a move on,' he said, looking up at Wilkinson. 'What now?'

WILKINSON'S OFFICE

The three children and Zorro almost filled Wilkinson's small office. What it lacked in size, it made up for with order. Wilkinson had taken a seat behind his desk, which was, as always, impeccably tidy. A pencil, a biro, a six-inch ruler and a stapler were neatly ordered by size beside a notepad, marked in neat copperplate handwriting with the date underlined with a straight line. He looked up at them, keenly.

'A few things to discuss, team. Firstly . . .' He paused, pulled open a drawer in his desk and drew out some pieces of paper held together with a blue string tag.

'Someone has been very bad,' he said, frowning at the paper. Jake swallowed nervously. Wilkinson shook his head gravely, not looking up from the paper.

'It seems *someone* has been acting against Embassy wishes. Somebody whose perfidious influence creeps into this very room . . . We can't be having our own private ambitions, can we?' A note of anger had crept into his voice.

Jake looked at Cora. Maybe the Embassy had heard about the secret mission that Tokelo Fortune had set them.

'It's just that—' he started, but Wilkinson held up a finger to silence him.

'We have systems for reasons. Challenges to those systems cannot be tolerated. The punishment will be severe.'

Jake bit his lip, waiting for the sentencing that seemed inevitable.

Wilkinson held up the papers and pointed to the blue string tag. 'Cases involving junior Undoers – such as you, Jake – should be bound with a red tag. Always red. Someone has been ignoring the filing guidelines. *Again.*' He sighed, oblivious to the children's relief. 'Which leads us to the business in hand.' He ran a finger down the list. 'In order of priority. Item one on the agenda. The serious one.

You seem to have broken contact with the Embassy?'

Jake exchanged further looks with Cora. The words of Tokelo Fortune that morning rattled through his brain. *I've taken the liberty of disabling their line of communication to you for multiple reasons.*

Multiple reasons?

Maybe one of the reasons had been to get them summoned to the Embassy.

Jake reached into his rucksack. 'The Mousephone isn't working,' he explained.

Wilkinson held out his hand and took the Necrommunicator from Jake. 'It's most unusual. Old magic is normally very reliable. Unfortunately, we still don't have the budget for a spectral phone, but we'll issue you with a replacement Necrommunicator by post as soon as possible.' He signed a slip of paper and put it in a neat tray of similar slips on his desk. 'It will be waiting for you on your return. The spectral postal service is very efficient in matters like this.'

'Great,' said Jake sarcastically. 'A dead mouse through the post.'

'Item two on the agenda. The child known as Sab.' He looked at Sab and Zorro and then at Sab again. 'I'm assuming you are Sab, is that correct?'

Sab gestured to Zorro. 'The only other option here is a fox . . . Of course I'm Sab.'

'Mr Sab, your new-found sensitivity to ghosts is both interesting and worrying to some at the Embassy. Sensitivity to ghosts does not *usually* develop for no reason . . . You'll need an examination, I'm afraid.'

Sab looked at Jake nervously. Wilkinson smiled disarmingly.

'Oh, no, no. It's nothing too serious. Basically, we just have to check that your soul is not being devoured from the inside by some kind of malevolent parasitic spectre.'

Sab went pale. 'A what?'

'It's surprisingly common . . . Now, where were we . . .?' Wilkinson's eyes flicked back to the paper. 'Ah, item three in priority.' He reached into the drawer again and pulled out a key. 'The keys to quarters. As an Undoer you'll probably be spending more time here – especially as your tolerance to being outside of your body grows.' He tossed the keys over to Jake, who immediately fumbled them on to the floor.

'Our own quarters?' said Jake, picking up the keys and picturing himself reclining on a sofa, playing computer games.

Wilkinson smiled. 'They're not the grandest, I'm afraid. Those are reserved for the senior Undoers. But I think you'll find them pleasing nonetheless.

'Last and most definitely least is item four on the agenda . . . A rather delicate subject . . . The strange case of the Wandering Wight you encountered at the ruined priory.'

Jake shuddered as Wilkinson continued.

'At first I thought our little mix-up earlier today was because of another filing error by my predecessor, Linda.'

Cora laughed humourlessly. 'And that's why Jake was nearly drained to nothingness by a Wandering Wight, instead of Undoing a harmless bird-watcher? A filing error?'

'Well . . .' Wilkinson smiled. 'It seems I may have been a little hasty laying the blame on Linda.'

Jake frowned. 'Then how come they got mixed up?'

Wilkinson scratched his head. 'I've done some unofficial investigations and it appears that somebody must have rewritten the file. The mix-up could only have happened as a deliberate act of malice.'

Jake blinked as Wilkinson picked up a neat pile of papers from his desk and shuffled them into an even neater pile.

'I think we're done, here, yes?'

Jake blinked. 'Erm . . . The small matter of a "deliberate act of malice" that almost got me sent to the Void!'

Wilkinson chuckled. 'It's just a theory at the moment, Jake. Just a theory. This Wandering Wight business is probably nothing to do with you. After all, you're incredibly insignificant in the grand scheme of things. I will investigate nevertheless.'

Jake glanced at Cora.

Wasn't it possible that this was something to do with him being the Chosen One? Could it be because he was currently tasked with assassinating the last remaining follower of Fenris?

Cora nudged him with her elbow. She knew what he was thinking. 'You always assume it's all about you, Jake,' she whispered.

Jake ignored her. He waved his hand at Wilkinson, who was now using a handkerchief to remove a speck of dust from the keyboard of the metal typewriter on his desk.

'Why else would someone tamper with the files? What does it mean?'

Wilkinson shrugged. 'I'm not exactly sure. It probably means nothing.' He paused and stood up, tucking the neat stack of papers beneath his arm.

'On an . . . erm . . . a completely different subject, Jake, do you know of anybody who might want you dead?'

The three children and Zorro followed Wilkinson through the Embassy, down a series of long corridors.

Sab nudged Jake. 'How big *is* this place?'

Wilkinson laughed. 'It's as big as it needs to be. Whilst it occupies a real building on the Earthly Plane, the Embassy of Dead takes up a much larger spectral footprint.'

Sab nodded, pretending to understand, then stepped to the side of the corridor to allow an elderly man to shuffle past. 'And all these people are dead?' he said a little too loudly.

Jake watched the old man slowly walk down the corridor. 'All apart from us, oh, and any other Undoers that happen to be here. Are there any Undoers here at the moment, Wilkinson?'

Wilkinson replied as he walked. 'Yes. They are being summoned as we speak. There's a special reception about to begin . . .' He stopped at a junction in the corridors. 'Here we are . . . How are your tickets doing?'

Jake glanced at his numbered ticket. '301,' he said.

Sab looked down at his. '86 . . . It's going down much faster.'

Wilkinson frowned. 'I'll arrange for Eustace to call you back to your body.' He reached into his pocket. 'Ah . . . I've left my spectral phone in my office. I'll need to go back.'

'What happens if you don't get there in time to phone him?' said Sab suspiciously.

'Your living body will die,' replied Wilkinson matter-of-factly. He pointed down the corridor. 'You're room 183.' He smiled proudly. 'We've taken the liberty of having your names engraved on the door.' He scratched his head. 'Now, where was I going?'

Sab goggled. 'You were about to phone Eustace to make sure he gets me back in my body before it dies!'

'That's it! I knew it was something important!'

Wilkinson spun on his heels and walked off in the opposite direction to where they had come from. Then he paused once more, spun on his heels and walked back past them in the right direction. 'It's like a rabbit warren. So many wrong turns,' he said, disappearing down the corridor.

BROOM CUPBOARD

'I was hoping they'd use my actual name,' said Jake.

The wooden door with the neat hand-painted sign read:

Wormling / Sanderford

Cora tutted. 'And the names are in the wrong order! *Sanderford / Wormling* reads so much better.' She looked at Jake, smiling in mock sympathy. 'It's also a more accurate reflection of our relationship.'

Jake returned her gaze, and he saw that beneath her freckly disdain for the sign on the door, she was secretly quite excited.

'Well, aren't you going to open it?' she asked. 'It's our very own office!'

Jake fumbled for the key. 'I'm glad you're not letting the little fact of someone wanting me dead spoil your enjoyment of this moment.'

But for once he shared her enthusiasm. He and Cora had been assigned their own quarters! He imagined a book-lined room and a leather desk. Maybe an oil portrait of Jake himself hanging above a roaring log fire . . . Oh, and an antique globe that opened to reveal some kind of secret fridge full of soft drinks and snacks. Actually, the fridge in a globe might be going too far. He'd settle for the portrait. Jake pushed the door open.

'It's a broom cupboard,' said Sab, chuckling to himself.

Jake looked around the windowless room. Even calling it a room was misleading. It was more of a windowless cell – barely big enough for them to both stand in. An old metal chair sat by a desk made from a piece of plywood bracketed to a peeling wall.

Sab picked out a dusty broom that leant against the wall.

'It literally *is* a broom cupboard. It's full of cleaning equipment.' He laughed, nudging a bucket with his toe.

There was a movement in the shadows behind

the bucket and then Sab shrieked as a large spider-like creature emerged from the darkness, scuttling across the floor then fading into nothingness.

Jake shuddered. 'It's Tokelo's Gomseer!' he said.

Cora scratched her head. 'Maybe Fortune's here. Didn't Wilkinson say there was a special reception? If he is, it looks like he's brought us something from the Afterworld.' She pointed to a package that was sitting on the desk. 'Another mysterious parcel.'

Jake frowned. 'It's the package Tokelo gave to the Gomseer!'

'Cool! It's like it's our birthday,' said Sab, reaching out for the package.

Jake pushed his hand away. 'Our birthday? Unfortunately it's addressed to me. Look.'

It had a paper label attached. The label simply read:

W.

Cora laughed. 'W for Wormling? You'd better open it.'

Sab laughed too. 'You've changed since you've become the Chosen One, Idiot. What happened to sharing everything? Please can I open it?'

Ignoring his friend, Jake opened the box carefully and lifted out an object that was wrapped in tissue paper, and placed it carefully on the table. Beneath the object was a handwritten note that read:

5.00 p.m.

You know what to do.

T

Jake dropped the note as it suddenly burst into flame. It disappeared with a puff of smoke, the only trace that it had ever existed a smudge of soot on Jake's fingers.

He looked at Cora in surprise. 'What's going on?' he groaned.

Cora's brow furrowed. 'T for Tokelo. Tokelo Fortune. *You know what to do.* It must be to do with . . .' She glanced over her shoulder cautiously, stepped into the room and closed the door behind her. Without the light from the corridor, the three children stood in the pitch black. 'Where's the light switch?' There was the sound of a mop being knocked over. Then a click and a naked bulb shone a dull flickering light over the trio. 'Even the lighting is dreadful.' Cora's voice lowered to a whisper. 'It must be to do with your mission,' she hissed. 'To send Arkus the Invincible to the Void.'

Jake shushed her. 'Don't say it. Saying it makes it seem real.'

'It *is* real. It's *your* destiny.'

He felt sick as he remembered Tokelo's words: *No, Jake, I'm expecting you to kill him.*

He wouldn't do it. He *couldn't* do it.

Once again, the safety of the world had been forced into his unwilling hands. And once again it seemed totally unfair.

He carefully unwrapped the object. Inside the tissue paper was a long shard of what looked like flint, chipped into two sharp points, one at the apex of the shard, a second halfway down one of the edges. A rounder shaft projected from the bottom of the flint, strapped tightly in leather cord . . . A handle? He glanced at Cora.

Sab peered over his shoulder. 'Great,' he said sarcastically. 'Happy birthday. Have a stone.'

Jake shook his head. He reached out for the shaft. It fitted into his hand as though it had been made for that very purpose. He held it up to the

95

flickering bulb, and the light shone dull through the brown stone.

He swallowed hard at the realisation of what he was holding. 'It's not a stone . . . It's a dagger.'

Cora's eyes opened wide. 'The weapon! The only weapon that can send Arkus the Invincible to the Eternal Void.'

Jake felt sick. 'Don't use the V-word.'

Cora tutted. 'This is what happens when the wrong sort of person is named in a prophecy,' she said.

Jake glared at her. 'Believe me. It's not just you who wishes that it was you and not me related to Uthred Dragon.'

For a moment there was a brooding silence.

'It is a cool name, isn't it? Uthred Dragon,' said Sab, immediately diffusing the tension. Jake smiled. Sometimes he thought Sab might be a master of diplomacy. He always said the right thing at the right time. Even if it was usually something silly.

Cora frowned. 'I've definitely heard that name somewhere before,' she said to herself.

Jake lifted the dagger. It was hard to believe such

a crude instrument could wield enough power to cut paper, let alone send a demon called Arkus the Invincible to the Eternal Void.

Cora shrugged. 'What's that bit for?'

At the widest part of the dagger – just above the hilt – was a triangular indentation. At first Jake thought it was a natural fault in the rock but now it seemed like it had been carefully carved. The shape was familiar. He pulled the tooth pendant from his hoodie, and looked at Cora.

It was the same size!

The following silence was broken by Sab. 'Well, aren't you going to put it in?'

'No.' Jake shook his head. 'I don't want any part of this.'

They stood there in silence for a bit. It was like time was waiting for them to do something. *Anything.* The tooth felt heavy around Jake's neck. The dagger felt cold.

'Do it!' Cora tempted him. 'It doesn't mean you have to send Arkus the Invincible to the Void. It might not even fit.'

Jake sighed. He knew it would.

Carefully he placed the knife back on the desk. Then, after untying the tooth from the necklace, he pressed it into the hole, where it slotted with a satisfying click.

'Aren't you going to pick it up?' whispered Cora. She reached out for the weapon.

Without thinking, Jake snatched it up before Cora had a chance to touch the hilt.

'Sorry,' he said. 'I don't know why I did that. Did you want to hold it?'

Cora raised an eyebrow. 'No. It's fine. Knock yourself out, Chosen One.'

Jake moved the dagger through the air. Once, when he had pulled the tooth through the air, it had snagged and cut a hole between the Earthly Plane and the Eternal Void. It was a hole that had sucked a plague demon to its demise. Now, the dagger – with the inset tooth – moved easily through the air, quicker than he expected, as if it had its own momentum. He lifted the blade to the sky. It felt strong. *He* felt strong.

A cold dread crept through his veins. He felt his pulse quicken. Steeling himself, he tightened his grip on the hilt, and for a second the shortness of breath and the feeling of panic were dispelled. He closed his eyes in relief, but instantly he was somewhere else – deep in a vision.

The room had shifted, the broom cupboard and his friends gone, to be replaced with a grisly scene like a single frame of a movie, hanging in time . . .

A figure lay before him on the ground, hidden beneath a cloak, its hand gripping something – a wooden model of a boat, as though the figure had grabbed at it as he'd fallen, and it had splintered and broken on impact with the floor. And where the blood soaked into the porous stone tiles, darkness grew, a still, oily blackness – the Eternal Void – and the figure started to slip, downwards into the darkness, sinking into the floor. Then the scene shifted, time moved forward and Jake could see his hand hovering over the disappearing figure. It seemed alien somehow, but it was his hand, it must be . . . He was holding the dagger – the weapon felt strange and alien, and something was staining his hands. And – just like that – in the blinking of an eye, the figure was gone, and Jake realised that it was Arkus, the heir to the

Kingdom of Demons. Jake knew that he had seen the
future. He had seen the moment when he sent Arkus
to the Eternal Void.

EUSTACE

ustace Carmichael-Bancombe tucked his Necrommunicator back into his pocket and shuddered. If he'd known that he'd have to carry a dead mouse around with his ghost, then he might have taken more care crossing the road all those years ago. Still, it was useful. Otherwise he would have no idea when to call back Jake or the other one whose name he'd forgotten already. Seb? Sam? Sab! That was it!

Within a couple of minutes, to be on the safe side, Wilkinson had said about Sab. Unlike Jake, Sab's sensitivity was weak to say the least. Eustace smiled proudly at the thought of Jake's growing power.

He would be an asset to the Embassy.

He glanced around the kitchen, then stepped into Jake's body. Eustace had no physical form, so to wake Sab and bring his spirit back to his body he needed to borrow one. Then Sab could wake Jake whenever necessary.

Eustace-in-Jake's-body waltzed over to the tap, slowly adjusting to Jake's shorter legs, and grimacing as he caught sight of his new face in the reflection of the kitchen window. That was the problem with being so handsome in his lifetime – cursed to spend his deathtime inhabiting the lesser bodies of others.

Still, not for long this time, though. He picked up a pint glass from the drying rack, noting that Jake's family actually had to do their own washing up.

'Poor fellows. I wouldn't know where to begin!' he said to himself in Jake's voice as he filled the glass with water.

Now he needed some ice. He opened the freezer section of the fridge. No ice but frozen peas would do to lower the temperature of the water. The packet was already open so he poured some peas into the water.

He whistled a tune to himself. It was from an operetta he had been fond of when he was a student.

Once he thought he might write his own musical, but now it was too late.

Now he had serious business to attend to. Business for the Embassy of the Dead.

He looked at Sab slumped in the chair. All he had to do was to throw the water in Sab's face.

Everything was going to plan, perfectly to plan.

There was the sound of the front door opening. Eustace froze.

'Hello?' came a voice from the hallway.

Jake's mother! She wandered in holding her coat.

'Hi, love, how was school?'

Eustace-in-Jake's-body jumped up. 'Allow me.' He took her coat and draped it over his arm.

Jake's mum looked at Eustace-in-Jake's-body through narrowed eyes. Then she turned and noticed Sab's body slumped in the chair over his phone.

'Hi, Sab,' she said.

Sab's empty body didn't answer.

Jake's mum tried again. 'Hi, Sab. How's your mum?'

There was still no reply.

'Sab?' she said again.

No response.

She tried once more. 'Sab?'

Still no reply.

Eustace-in-Jake's-body closed his eyes in dismay. Any second now, Jake's mum would realise that there was the lifeless body of a child sitting in a chair in her kitchen.

'Bloody kids and their phones,' she muttered, picking up the kettle to make a cup of tea.

TIME TO KILL

'**J**ake!'

It was Cora.

Jake shook his head to clear his brain.

'Someone's at the door!' she hissed. 'Quick! The dagger. Hide it.'

Jake blinked. 'I saw something . . . A vision.'

A look of concern flashed across Cora's face. 'You've gone pale.'

Jake nodded and gazed at the flint blade. 'I think I saw something from my future. The knife . . . I . . .'

The knocking sounded again.

'Are you in there, Wormling?' It was the voice of Wilkinson. The handle started to turn and the door banged into Sab. He pressed his back against it.

'Just a second. There's not much room in here!'

Cora leant forward. 'You had a premonition of your destiny,' she whispered in awe.

Jake dropped the dagger on the desk and Cora quickly picked up a dustpan and placed it over the weapon. She turned and, pushing Sab to one side, opened the door, smiling sweetly at Wilkinson. 'We need to talk about our quarters,' she said.

Wilkinson looked around the tiny room. His eyes rested on Sab. 'What are you still doing here?'

Sab looked at his ticket. 'It says 12. Is that bad?'

Wilkinson frowned. 'I told Eustace to summon you within minutes.' He glanced at his wristwatch. '4.45 p.m.,' he muttered. Wilkinson scratched his head. 'No matter. I'm sure Eustace has it in hand.' He beamed proudly at Cora, motioning around the broom cupboard. 'Such charming quarters!' he proclaimed. 'Are you pleased?'

Cora shook her head in disbelief. 'It's a cupboard.'

Wilkinson nodded. 'Yes. It's amazing what you can do with a little bit of imagination.' He turned to Jake. 'And how long do you have left?'

Jake gulped.

5 p.m. You know what to do.

'Until what?' he croaked.

'Before your time at the Embassy runs out, of course. There's something I'd like to show you.'

Jake looked at his ticket. 286.

'The number's ticking down more slowly than normal,' he said.

Wilkinson scratched his head. 'It appears your tolerance to being out of your body has increased significantly quicker than is usual. We'd expect some improvement due to your repeated visits but this is astounding . . .'

Cora yawned theatrically. 'Yes. We know. Jake is very gifted.'

Jake glanced at Cora but missed her gaze. His hand snuck to the pendant – but of course, it was no longer around his neck. It didn't feel right – the tooth not being on him. He felt weaker, somehow. His hand began to creep out towards the desk.

Cora scowled at him, took the broom from Sab and leant it against the wall, putting herself between him and the weapon.

'You wanted to show us something, Mr Wilkinson?' She wiped a finger along the desk towards the dustpan, and Jake's heart leapt into his mouth. Was she going to pick up the weapon herself?

Instead she showed her grimy finger to Wilkinson. 'I'm quite keen on getting out of this dirty cupboard.'

Wilkinson bounced on his heels. 'Yes, I've a surprise for you all . . .'

Cora wiped her grimy finger on Sab. 'Before we go, can I just check it isn't some kind of new stationery?'

Wilkinson laughed and began to pace down the corridor. 'No. Although I have just received a delivery of a classic 1980s hole punch if you'd like me to show you.'

Quickly Jake shifted the dustpan. On the desk lay the weapon. He paused for a second, looking at it, then swept it into his rucksack, before turning and trotting down the corridor after the others. It was safest that it was with them, even if it definitely wasn't going to be used.

Wilkinson led them through the Embassy via a labyrinth of corridors, nooks and mysterious doors. Eventually, they joined a wide corridor ended by an open pair of double doors flanked either side by a smartly dressed footman, each holding a tray of drinks.

Sab went to take a glass of champagne and the footman raised the tray out of his reach.

Wilkinson guided Sab through the door. 'Today the Embassy is honoured with a special guest. In a way, you're lucky that Eustace has delayed recalling you to your body. A happy coincidence, you might say.' He clapped his hands together, unable to conceal his excitement any longer. 'It's a once-in-a-deathtime opportunity.'

Wilkinson led Jake, Cora and Sab into an elegant ballroom. There was a large gathering of official-looking people all milling around. 'What's the reason for the celebration?' Cora said.

'It's in honour of the Ministry of Security. After you successfully thwarted the plot to unsettle the Afterworld – and exposed the Captain's treachery – the Ministry acted swiftly to clear the hornets' nest, so to speak.' He sighed with relief. 'They arrested all the remaining demons and ghosts who were loyal to Fenris. The Afterworld is safe for the foreseeable future.'

Sab leant behind Jake. 'All but one!' he whispered.

'What's that?' asked Wilkinson.

Sab scratched his chin. 'It seems like fun,' he said, thinking on his feet. He gestured at the stiff-looking crowd.

Jake had been at a party for ghosts before, but this was a different – altogether more formal – affair. Through the crowd, his eyes caught the gaze of a tall, thin-faced woman. She smiled at him and he turned away, embarrassed at the unexpected eye-contact.

Zorro growled.

'What is it, Zorro?' said Jake, taking the opportunity of Zorro's solidity to give him a scratch behind the ear.

Zorro looked at him and Jake picked him up for the first time, cradling him like a baby in his arms.

'What's up?' asked Sab, distractedly. He was toying with his ticket.

Wilkinson put his hand on Sab's shoulder. 'It will be fine. Eustace is one of our best. Whatever problem has caused him to delay your recall will soon be solved, I'm sure.'

Sab looked at Jake. 'I hope so. I'm not ready for the . . . Afterworld yet.'

Jake stood on tiptoes, trying to find the lady who had smiled at him. She had seemed familiar, somehow. Then he saw her again. She was standing next to another lady, slightly older but obviously her sister. The same shabby clothes, the same pinched face, and curved nose – a bit like the beak of a bird of prey. Then he remembered.

The older lady was a senior Undoer, the younger lady her spectral assistant. They'd been at his initiation ceremony, sitting on the stage. Someone had told him they were twins. One had died while young. The other had lived.

He nudged Cora, who was holding a plate of canapés.

'Who are *they* again?' he whispered. 'They were at my initiation ceremony.'

Wilkinson was standing behind them. He looked over to the sisters. 'You've not heard of the Mittle sisters?' he said. 'The Mittle Affair was famous when I was alive. Perhaps, though, you are too young.'

Jake shrugged. 'Probably.'

Wilkinson continued, not tearing his eyes away from the sisters. 'Agnes and Nancy Mittle. Twin daughters of a retired Austrian military man. A most interesting ethical dilemma: both of them caught in a snowstorm in the Alps, shortly after attending the reading of their father's will. Of course, it's all gossip but apparently they were holed up in a cabin for a week before making the decision that one of them should fetch help while the other should stay put in case a search party found them. They drew lots and the younger twin, Nancy, left.' Wilkinson looked at the ground. 'By chance a search party arrived at the cabin mere minutes later, but poor Nancy was never seen again.' He paused for effect before continuing brightly. 'Well, not until her ghost showed up. Now the surviving sister, Agnes, is an Undoer and Nancy the ghost sister is her assistant.'

Jake glanced back at the sisters. Now the older – living – one was looking at him, frowning from across the ballroom floor. Jake turned away, unable to hold her stare. 'Why are they looking at me?' said Jake. It was making him uneasy.

Wilkinson shrugged. 'You certainly seem to have piqued their interest, Jake.'

Cora laughed and nudged Jake sharply. 'Maybe they remember you from your initiation ceremony, *Wormling*. So embarrassing for you.'

Jake rubbed his arm where Cora had elbowed him and was about to complain about her taking full advantage of her newfound solidity when he caught sight of Tokelo Fortune, his head tucked beneath his arm, standing on a balcony that wrapped around the room above them.

'Look!' he hissed.

Cora's eyes followed his gaze. 'Tokelo Fortune. He's with the Ambassador.'

'That explains the Gomseer!' Jake whispered back.

One of the dignitaries on the balcony shifted, revealing the small form of the Ambassador of the Embassy of the Dead in her tweedy jacket, jodhpurs and riding jacket.

Sab looked up. He'd overheard their whispers. 'Tokelo Fortune? Is that the guy who wants you to . . .' He stopped short at the pained expression on

Jake's face. 'Erm . . . who wants you to be called Wormling.' He scratched his nose innocently.

At the end of the ballroom was a grand flight of stairs, at the top of which the balcony ran along the room. Halfway along this balcony Tokelo Fortune was chatting to the Ambassador with a broad grin across his face. Even the Ambassador of the Embassy of the Dead, usually a glowering lady, seemed in a good mood. Then something caught her eye and she broke off from the conversation. The hush spread across the room and Jake turned to see why everyone had stopped talking.

One of the footmen who had been at the door now stood at the top of the stairs.

'Ladies, gentlemen, dead and living, wraiths, spectres, and Wights. Please stand for the entrance of Prince Arkus the Invincible . . .'

Somewhere a clock struck five times, a noise that went unheard to most of the gathered ghosts and living people outside of their bodies. But not to Jake.

5 o'clock.

It was time.

ARKUS THE INVINCIBLE

T he footman stood to the side and a figure appeared at the top of the stairs, no taller than Jake, dressed in a suit and tie, with a long yellow cloak trailing in his wake. It was a child. A normal-looking child – if you ignored the clothes – blinking out at the gathered dignitaries through round spectacles.

Behind him he heard Wilkinson's voice, breathless and full of wonderment. 'Behold Arkus the Invincible, prince of demons.'

The child prince held his hand in the air, and a small ripple of applause started, slowly becoming louder. The prince shuffled on his feet and smiled shyly at the crowd, running a hand nervously through his curly hair to reveal a pair of growths like small horns above his forehead.

'He's got devil antlers growing!' said Sab.

A ghost in a ball gown turned around and glared at Sab.

Wilkinson gave Sab a stern look. 'Technically they're ossicones, not antlers. They won't get any bigger,' said Wilkinson. 'And he's a demon not a devil. Different things.'

'Ossicones. Who'd have thought?' murmured Sab. 'What the heck are ossicones?'

Wilkinson smiled. 'They're small horns. Like a giraffe's . . .'

Jake shut his ears to the chatter. It was like he was watching a bad dream unfold in front of him. This was Arkus. This was the demon he was supposed to kill. He turned to Wilkinson. 'But he's a kid?'

Wilkinson was a bit shocked. 'Of course he's a child. He's barely two hundred!'

Cora scratched her head. 'Why is he called the *Invincible*? He doesn't seem invincible to me. Looks like he'd blow over in a light breeze.'

Wilkinson nodded. 'Ah, of course . . . You are not aware that all of the demons with royal blood are invincible. They cannot be killed. They cannot *even* be sent to the Void!'

Tokelo Fortune's words echoed round Jake's head. He bit his lip to prevent himself saying them aloud.

Fenris' tooth . . . *a reaper's tooth* . . . could send the prince to the Void! The very same tooth that at this moment sat implanted in a stone dagger in his rucksack.

He exchanged a nervous glance with Cora, as the child-demon started to walk down the stairs, pausing at each step to greet the assembled guests who surged upwards to meet him.

Wilkinson was still talking. '. . . his father can travel between the Earthly Plane and the Afterworld at will . . . Much like a reaper.'

'And that kid can do that too?' asked Sab.

It seemed so unlikely that this 'kid' had any special powers at all.

'I think it's likely he's not yet mastered his ability. It's a learnt skill – adapted from their particular demon type's panic reflex. In moments of extreme danger they will disappear and reappear somewhere else – usually, somewhere they have a connection to, like a safe space or a place with happy memories – in either the Earthly Plane or the Afterworld. With training, this reflex can be controlled. The king uses it to travel around his kingdom in the Afterworld and occasionally to visit the Embassy of the Dead. The prince, however, will have crossed by the bridge.'

Jake nodded. He had used the bridge between the two worlds before. Wilkinson took a canapé from a passing waiter and popped it into his mouth.

'They say when the royal demons are younglings, they have to bind them to their bed with Enchanted Deathweed – an Afterworld plant – to stop them slipping to another location every time they cry!' He brushed some flaky pastry crumbs from his shirt.

'How does that work?' asked Cora.

Wilkinson shrugged. 'Deathweed is an interesting plant. It has strange properties. One of these is the neutralisation of what you might call "demon magic". It's a defence mechanism. Similar to a blackberry bush having thorns to prevent you picking all its fruit.'

'Pretty cool, though, huh?' said Sab. 'Just travelling wherever you want. Teleporting here and there.' He held up his ticket. 'Talking of flitting between worlds . . .'

Wilkinson didn't seem to hear. 'Like all powers, it comes with great responsibility and is not to be abused,' he continued. 'It's lucky the royal demons are so respected in the Afterworld by demons and the dead alike.' He looked at Sab. 'Also, I'm led to believe it uses a lot of spirit energy. For a demon as young as the prince, even a single jump could leave him weak.'

Jake clenched his teeth as the demon Arkus continued working his way through the crowd, greeting the adult dead with a nervous handshake.

Wilkinson stooped and whispered into Jake's ear. 'He's incredibly considerate. He'll insist on meeting everyone. Not one of those brooding, stand-offish demon types, you'll be pleased to know.' He smiled proudly. 'Like his father, Arkus believes the work of the Embassy is crucially important to the functioning of the Afterworld Authorities and the continuing peace between demons and the dead.'

Wilkinson looked thoughtful for a second. 'Of course . . . his father's life is coming to an end, five thousand years is a good innings. He's been a just king for demonkind, and true in his determination to keep peace between the demons and the dead.' He smiled. 'We're confident that Prince Arkus will live up to his father's legacy and continue his good work.'

Jake swallowed hard.

Tokelo Fortune had said that the Embassy knew nothing of Arkus's loyalty to Fenris the fallen reaper. And Jake could see that this at least was true. Everybody was bowing or curtsying, as the demon prince exchanged a few words with them.

Jake glanced at Cora. 'We've got to get out of here. I can't do it,' he whispered.

Cora looked concerned. 'And your destiny?'

'I can't do it,' repeated Jake. 'I just can't.'

'I mean, this is your chance . . . Your chance to make your family known throughout history. Don't you want that? It's the sort of thing I was taught was important. The family name and all that . . .'

Jake shook his head. 'Not really.'

Cora shrugged. 'Let's get out of here then. See if

we can get Wilkinson to send us home. This party's pretty tame, anyway.'

Jake turned to follow but his feet felt like lead. He suddenly felt anxious. Like the weapon and the tooth were missing. Like they'd fallen from the rucksack, somehow. Even though he was *sure* he had zipped it securely.

'Wait!' he said, dropping to his knees and removing his rucksack from his back to check. Cora and Sab turned around.

It was as though the weapon was calling to him. Jake felt his own hand moving like a spider through his bag, feeling for the stone blade.

'My destiny . . .' he whispered. A sense of relief flooded his body as his fingers wrapped around the hilt.

He felt Cora's hand grab him, pulling him to his feet. 'Jake, what's wrong? You've gone all weird.' Her voice sounded muffled. Distant.

'It is time. . .' he heard himself say.

His fingers tightened their grip.

He felt strong. It was time for his destiny to be fulfilled.

'Jake!'

Jake blinked. For a moment the fog cleared. Cora was standing before him, and Sab. He saw their concern for him.

He thought of his mum and dad.

Jake felt himself break free of whatever hold was upon him. He felt the blood rush to his face. He turned to Cora. 'For a moment I wasn't in control. I wasn't in control of my body.' He breathed. 'I was going to do it!'

He looked up for Tokelo Fortune but the Minister of Security was nowhere to be seen.

Jake felt a tap on his shoulder, and turned around to find himself facing the demon prince. Wilkinson was beside him, smiling like a happy child.

'And this, Your Majesty, is Wormling. He's our youngest Undoer.'

Jake stood open-mouthed, clutching his rucksack tightly to his chest, his hand still tucked inside.

'You're supposed to bow, Wormling,' said Cora, executing a perfect curtsy. 'It's like you've never met a royal before . . .'

'Sorry, Your W-worshipfulness. I mean Your M-majesty,' Jake stuttered.

He was about to bow when he felt a huge blow to his side that sent him spinning forward. He jerked his hand from the rucksack, instinctively reaching out for something that would break his fall. He felt the fingers of his free hand grip the soft yellow fabric of the prince's cloak, and heard him cry as he too tumbled to the floor. Then he heard shouting.

'Treachery! He has a blade!'

And another shout: 'The Wormling has a knife!'

He felt hands upon him, gripping his hoodie. He heard Cora's voice shouting, 'Get off him, get off him!'

He looked down and saw that he was lying upon the fallen body of the prince, who was staring up at him with a scared expression. Zorro, too, was tangled in the folds of the prince's cloak.

He felt a hand on his shoulder and, turning, he saw the figure of the older, living Mittle sister, Agnes, kneeling beside him. Her bony hand gripped his wrist, her fingers digging into his flesh. 'He has the demon-slayer's blade!'

Jake looked down. The hilt of the blade was still held firmly in his hand. He turned back to Arkus. 'I . . . I . . . wasn't g-going to . . .' stuttered Jake. He paused at the expression of shock on the demon prince's face. Like he was struggling for breath. The prince clawed at his throat.

'Are you OK . . .?' began Jake.

The prince's eyes rolled to the back of his head, and then a hole appeared around him, like a perfectly circular area of floor had just fallen through into a dark chasm, and he fell. For a split second Jake just lay there watching Arkus's cloak slip through the floor.

'Zorro!'

The fox slid past him, tangled in the yellow fabric of the prince's cloak. Jake reached out for the fox but the grip of Agnes Mittle was too strong on his wrist. Jake watched helplessly as Zorro disappeared.

Then he too was enveloped by the hole. He felt his wrist slipping through the fingers of Agnes and Jake was falling into darkness, falling after the demon prince.

'Jake!'

It was Cora. He felt the hook of her hockey stick catch in his hood, jerking him to halt in mid-air, choking him, and then he heard her swear, and he felt himself falling again and in the darkness he reached out and caught hold of a hand. Cora's hand. And now both he and Cora were falling through the darkness together.

I n the corner of the kitchen, Sab's spiritless
body still sat slumped on the chair. Jake's
mum looked at Eustace-in-Jake's-body over the
rim of a mug of steaming hot tea.

'So . . . are you going to tell me what you're up
to, young man?' she said, taking a sip.

Eustace-in-Jake's-body blinked. She was good.
She could read that something wasn't right. Maybe
he hadn't got Jake's posture quite correct. Often,
the living would subconsciously block out the
little things that confused them, but Jake's mum
seemed to be rather astute. Eustace-in-Jake's-body
readjusted the way he was standing, relaxing his
back into a slouch.

'I'm not sure I understand, Mother . . . Mum,' he
replied, glancing at the clock. Sab didn't have very

long left before his body would die. Wilkinson had said a few minutes . . .

'I mean, why are you drinking a glass of peas?' she asked.

Eustace-in-Jake's-body looked at the glass in his hand. He panicked. 'Oh this. A mere fancy!'

Jake's mum frowned. She opened her mouth to say something when the doorbell rang.

'Shall I get the door then?' she said, after a moment of neither of them moving.

Eustace held Jake's breath. 'That would be most convenient.'

She gazed at him suspiciously then left the kitchen to walk to the front door. The second she'd disappeared from view, Eustace spun round to face Sab's body.

There was the sound of the door opening. Then closing. Then Jake's mum's voice sounded from the hallway. 'No one there. But there's a package for you. What have you been ordering online?'

She sounded cross. Throwing a glass of water over Sab probably wouldn't help that particular problem but it had to be done. It was, quite literally, a matter of life and death.

'It's for Father . . . Dad,' he lied, thinking on his feet. 'A surprise present.'

'It's not his birthday until August!' replied Mum.

Eustace swore to himself.

'That's why it's a surprise?'

'Oh.' She paused for a moment – presumably to think – and it was just long enough for Eustace-in-Jake's-body to take a deep breath and lift the glass above Sab's head . . .

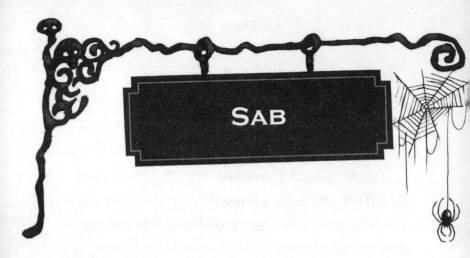

SAB

Sab watched in horror as his friends disappeared through the floor. As if slowly running out of time to be outside of your body wasn't bad enough, being the sole remaining member of a recently discovered plot to assassinate a demon prince was even worse.

A crowd had gathered around the empty patch of floor through which they'd all disappeared. Now they parted, and the Ambassador stepped forward and rapped her boot heel against the wooden floor. It was solid once more.

'It seems the prince has triggered his panic reflex. We can't be sure where he'll end up. It could be either in the Afterworld or the Earthly Plane. He may not be able to control his final destination like his father but the panic reflex will take him somewhere with a personal connection.'

A lady with a clipboard appeared at her side, taking notes. 'Anything else, ma'am?'

The Ambassador frowned. 'Yes, Maureen, send Mawkins to Wormling's house. It's possible they will end up there. Wormling's presence in the fall may affect the destination.'

'Mawkins, ma'am? Yes, ma'am.'

The gathered crowd fell silent as Maureen strode off.

Sab didn't know who Mawkins was but anybody whose name preceded a sudden silence like that didn't sound like the sort of person you'd want sent to your best friend's house.

The Ambassador continued. 'And summon the Undoers. We need to cover all locations if and when they surface in the Earthly Plane.' She cracked her riding crop angrily against her open palm. 'We need to know all the details.' Slowly she turned to face Sab. 'Tell us all you know or face extremely undesirable circumstances.'

Sab gulped. He looked at his ticket. It said two. He was almost stuck in the Embassy without a living body to return to.

'Well . . .' he began and at that very moment he disappeared from the Embassy of the Dead.

CATCHING RATS

It turned out that falling into darkness did strange things to Jake's mind. For the first minute or so, Jake's body was tensed and rigid – bracing itself for the inevitable impact. As he spiralled through the air Cora's hand slipped from his and he screamed, and the scream seemed like it wouldn't end, until finally his breath ran out and it died in his throat with a whimper, only to be picked up again as soon as he had taken another breath. Then this second scream died too. Jake's body had stopped spinning and he was falling, spreadeagled like a skydiver. He could feel the wind buffeting his body and with its presence came a feeling of calmness. Of acceptance . . . Somewhere below him he could see a shape. Another person. Arkus. Falling faster than him, spinning away.

I am going to die, he thought, accepting the inevitable result of falling. He closed his eyes.

And then after another minute, Jake's calmness was replaced by mild irritation.

How long is this going to go on for?

And then by boredom.

Why am I not—

Which is when he hit the ground, landing on his front, still spread out like a human-starfish hybrid, the air forced from his lungs. For a while he lay there – face down – in a puddle of wetness he hoped was water. He sat up and felt himself for broken bones. He was sitting in a dark concrete passageway. Standing, he surveyed his surroundings. The wetness that had now soaked the seat of his jeans like an embarrassing accident did appear to be water. It was dripping down the walls and gathering into a small gutter that trickled past his feet – the permanence of its course marked by green algal streaks on the bare concrete walls. He looked down the passage-way. In one direction the corridor bent to the left, a shaft of light indicating that somewhere around the corner there was a window perhaps. The other

way disappeared through some smashed-up doors
into a similarly grim stairwell.

Where am I?

He gazed at his hands. He was solid – for what
that was worth. The possibilities revolved around his
head. It meant he was either still in the Embassy of
the Dead, or he was back in his body.

The last thing he had known was that he was
falling. Falling into nothing.

Cora had been there! Something caught his eye,
the shadow of something lying across the gutter. A
stick. A hockey stick!

He rushed forward.

'Cora!' The word fell from his mouth and echoed
around the enclosed concrete.

'Missing me, Precious?' came a voice from just
around the corner.

Jake ran along the corridor. Daylight was coming
from a crack in a boarded-up window. Standing
astride the filthy gutter below it, brushing herself
down, was Cora.

Jake sighed with relief. 'I'm glad to see you!'

Cora didn't repay the compliment.

He blinked. 'You're still solid!'

She looked down at herself. 'So I am. Where are we?' She picked up her boater from the floor and shook it. Tiny droplets of water flicked over Jake.

'Somewhere damp,' said Jake. 'What happened?'

Cora laughed. 'You mean after you fell on the prince or before?' She stopped laughing. 'You were bundled to the floor by one of the terrible twins. It was like they knew you had something in your bag.'

'B-but I-I wasn't going to do anything . . .' Jake stammered. 'I couldn't.'

'I know,' said Cora. 'You don't have the stomach for it.' She inspected her nails. 'Arkus just fell through the door – like a trapdoor had opened – and he took you with him. I hooked you with my stick but tumbled in after you. We all fell together.'

Jake looked around nervously. 'He should be around here somewhere, then.' His heart jumped. 'What about Zorro?'

Cora rubbed her chin thoughtfully. The last thing I need is another dumb animal to take care of . . .' She paused. 'Oh.'

Zorro padded round the corner.

She stooped down to rub his ears, then looked up at Jake. 'Do you think he heard me?'

Jake smiled. 'I don't think he cares.' He gazed round again at their surroundings. Wherever they were, it didn't seem promising.

But at least they were all in it together. Jake was just thinking how to verbalise this sentiment in a way that wouldn't make Cora laugh at him, when he heard the slapping sound of footsteps in the wet passageway and a figure turned the corner, pushing a wheelbarrow.

The figure, a wiry man with greying hair and dressed only in a filthy tunic, hardly gave them a glance as he trundled past, his face greased with fresh sweat from the exertion of pushing his barrow. Jake cast his eyes down at its strange cargo. Rats. Hundreds of dead rats, bundled in groups of about ten and tied by the tail. He looked at Cora as the man continued on his way.

'Excuse me,' Cora called out to the man's back.

The man stopped and carefully lowered the wheelbarrow. Then he turned to face them. 'Doesn't do any good to play in the Lowers of Deadhaven.' He shook his head sadly. ''Tis no place for children.'

'Deadhaven!' Cora exchanged a glance with Jake. She gripped her hockey stick tightly. 'We're in the Afterworld!'

Jake nodded. He'd seen Deadhaven before. From the hill on the edge of the Eternal Void its lights had sparkled in the night.

Jake closed his eyes in dismay. 'We need to get back, Sab might be in trouble.'

The man looked confused. 'But you're dead. No other reason you'd be in the Afterworld.' He narrowed his eyes. 'I got suspicions you might be playing a child's game on me . . . Having fun at the expense of old Harry Rat-catcher.' He turned to the window and forced his fingers between the boarding. With a tug, and the sound of rotten wood coming away from rusty nails, the passageway flooded with the dim evening light.

Jake and Cora stared through the gap in the planks and their eyes were drawn upwards. It seemed like they were near the bottom of a huge complex of tightly packed tower blocks that stretched up high

into the sky, their tops disappearing in cloud and their lower reaches plunging into an interminable darkness.

The old man smiled. 'The towers of Deadhaven! Well, you're certainly on the wrong floor. And it isn't the place for the asking of questions . . .' His eyes shifted around nervously. 'Or the answering . . .' He ran the back of his hand across his sweaty brow. 'But if I were you, I'd try to find your families, and if you're lucky they'll be the types that live higher up.' He smiled ruefully. 'I don't suppose you want to buy a rat?'

Jake shook his head. 'I don't have any money.'

Cora stared at him. 'But you would buy some if you had?' she whispered incredulously.

The rat-catcher cleared his throat and spat on the floor. 'I didn't spend the last two hundred years working my way up from the lower levels to spend time explaining myself to you tourists,' he said. Once more he peered through the split boards. Jake looked down with him into the darkness.

'See that down there, boy?' said the rat-catcher.

'See what?' asked Jake.

'Exactly!' the rat-catcher replied. 'Some of us ain't lucky enough to start off at the top levels. Some of us start right at the bottom. It's taken me two centuries to work my way up to here, and God knows, I can't face going much higher. I'm staying here, with my trade.' He paused and patted a bushel of rats. 'And my customers in the market.' He pointed down the corridor. 'So if you don't mind, I'll be heading on my way.'

And with a grunt, the rat-catcher picked up his wheelbarrow, and trundled off down the corridor.

'So we're here again,' said Cora, joining Jake at the window and looking out at the city that climbed downwards to darkness and upwards into the sky.

'The Afterworld.' Jake shook his head. He felt her eyes boring into him and he turned to face her, surprised by the excitement on her face. 'What is it?'

'You know what this means, don't you?' she asked.

'Nope,' Jake replied.

'It means . . .' She paused for dramatic effect. 'It means you're dead!'

Jake shook his head. 'I don't feel dead.'

'How do you know what dead feels like, if you haven't died?' asked Cora.

'Exactly . . . If I was dead, I'd know what it feels like and I don't know what it feels like so I can't be dead.'

Cora looked puzzled. 'I think we should go back to me being the smart one,' she said after a moment's silence. 'And anyway, even if you're not dead, you're still in big trouble. *We're* in big trouble.'

Jake looked through the ripped boards. Outside the sun was beginning to set over the city. 'Only a few people know Arkus is a follower of Fenris and even though I wasn't going to kill him people think I tried.'

Cora shrugged. 'Everyone at the Embassy seemed very fond of him, don't you think?'

Jake stared at Cora in horror. 'They'll think I tried to kill the next king of the demons. Like I'm some sort of crazed assassin!'

Cora slapped him on the back. 'On the bright side, you also *didn't* manage to kill the last remaining follower of Fenris.'

He groaned and sank his head into his hands. 'Sarcasm is the lowest form of humour.' He ran a hand through his hair. 'I'm in so much trouble! And you too.'

Cora thought for a bit. 'We need to get help. From Tokelo Fortune. Or someone else from the Ministry of Security – someone that knows we were on an official mission.'

Jake rubbed the back of his head. 'And until then we need to stay clear of anybody that might want to send us to . . .' He could hardly bring himself to say it.

'The Void?' asked Cora, casually juggling a broken piece of brick on her hockey stick.

Jake nodded. 'Basically we need to lie low and work out how to get back.'

Cora squatted on the floor to pick up a piece of paper that had fluttered from Jake's bag. The cloakroom ticket from the Embassy of the Dead. She held it up to Jake and he took it from her in time to see the number change from 98 to 97.

He groaned again. 'We might not have time for lying low.'

Cora tilted her head to one side. 'Did you hear that?'

Jake shook his head. 'What?'

'Someone calling for help.'

Jake listened carefully. After a short wait, a voice sounded. High-pitched, frightened. 'Help!'

Cora gripped her hockey stick.

'Someone's in trouble,' he said. 'Do you think we should—'

But Cora was already running off down the corridor in the direction of the shouts, with Zorro yapping at her heels.

FROZEN PEAS

Sab jumped up from the chair in Jake's mum's kitchen. 'I had nothing to do with anything. I don't even know Jake . . .' He blinked at Eustace-in-Jake's-body. 'Jake?'

'It's me, Eustace,' whispered Eustace, pressing a finger to his lips and pointing to the kitchen door. 'Mother's back!' he warned.

Sab's eyes opened in horror. He took a second and composed himself. He felt his face, and then looked down his front. 'I'm soaking . . .' he began. Then he remembered. 'It's Jake, he's disappeared! I think he's in serious trouble!'

Eustace opened his mouth to reply.

'Who's in serious trouble?' said Jake's mum, coming back into the room. She turned to Eustace-in-Jake's-body, who was standing over Sab with an empty pint glass. 'I've left that package on the hall table . . .' She frowned. 'Have you poured a glass of frozen peas in water over Sab?'

Eustace-in-Jake's-body picked up a nearby tea towel and tossed it to Sab. 'Awfully sorry. I tripped.'

Sab dried his hair on the faded tea towel. It was one of those ones you get from schools with a self-portrait of every child printed across it. He found Jake's self-portrait from year 3. 'Just as weird-looking back then.' Sab chuckled, glancing at Jake's body across the table. 'Idiot.'

'I say. You've a pea in your hair, Sab.'

Sab picked out a frozen pea and flicked it from a distance into the sink. He glared. 'Why are you still doing that weird posh accent we were practising for that play?' he said, glaring at Eustace-in-Jake's-body meaningfully. *Remember you're a kid.*

Jake's mum looked up. 'Oh! What play is that?'

Eustace wracked his brain for a plausible response. The kind of answer that Jake would really give his mum. He shrugged. 'Dunno,' said Eustace-in-Jake's-body. Sab nodded approvingly.

Jake's mum shook her head and walked out of

the room.

Sab took a deep breath. 'This is too weird.' He paused, looking at the tea towel. 'Not as weird as year 3 Jake's face, though.' He dropped the towel in a heap on the floor. Then he turned to Eustace-in-Jake's-body. 'Jake and Cora are in serious trouble. The Scary Horse lady thinks they tried to kill Prince Airbus the Invincible.'

Eustace-in-Jake's-body raised an eyebrow. At least he would have if Jake's facial muscles could manage such a feat; instead he simply twitched. 'You'd better start at the very beginning, Sab,' he said, glancing at the door to make sure Jake's mum was out of hearing range.

'Jake fell through a hole in the floor. Well, it wasn't a hole really . . . We need to get him. He's in danger,' Sab blurted.

Eustace held up his hand for silence and gazed intently at Sab. 'We'll summon him back to his body.' He pointed over to the kitchen counter. 'Fill that jug with water.'

Sab turned around, beaming. 'I get to throw a jug of water in Jake's face?'

Eustace nodded. 'Yes. I thought you might enjoy that.'

Sab reached into the fridge and pulled out a plate wrapped in cellophane.

Jake's trout dinner. 'Can I not just hit you round the face with this cold, dead fish?'

Eustace frowned. 'I'm not sure. It's never been tried. The official technique to summon a spirit back to its body is . . .' He looked at Sab, who had started filling the jug. 'I see you were making some sort of humorous comment.' His eyes sparkled. 'You know what, old chap. In another life we might have been friends. I'm sure we would have come up with some splendid—'

That's when Sab threw the water in his face. 'SURPRISE!' he shouted.

He watched as Eustace-in-Jake's-body blinked through the water. For a second the two stood staring into each other's eyes.

'Jake,' said Sab. 'Are you back?'

There was a brief pause and then Jake replied in Eustace's unmistakable tone. 'Oh, dear boy. I'm afraid something has *not* gone to plan.' Eustace-still-

148

in-Jake's-body collapsed backwards into a kitchen chair and pushed Jake's wet hair away from his eyes. His lip quivered, then he composed himself. 'This is no good. No good at all. In fact, I'm not sure how things could get much worse than this.'

Sab scratched his head.

Then he remembered something he'd heard just after Jake, Cora and Zorro disappeared through the floor after the prince.

'And who's this Mawkins guy they're sending here to pick them up?'

The blood drained from Eustace-in-Jake's-body's face. His eyes opened very wide. 'It just got worse,' he croaked. 'Much worse!'

Prince Arkus

Jake caught up with Cora and Zorro at a pair of old doors hanging off their hinges. Squeezing through a gap led them to a concrete stairwell. A small stream trickled down the stairs in a sequence of tiny waterfalls.

'Which way?' Jake gasped, catching his breath.

There was another cry, shriller this time – coming from above them.

Cora pointed upwards with her hockey stick. 'This way!' she shouted, leaping up the stairs three at a time.

Jake followed and found her on the next landing, looking through a doorway open to the outside.

Leading from the doorway was a rope-bridge spanning the twenty-metre gap between the tower they were in and another, similar tower. The view over Deadhaven was amazing. From the doorway Jake could see hundreds of towers reaching into the sky, the occasional lights of their windows merging with the stars that were beginning to peek through the twilight sky. The rope-bridge looked strange and out of place between the two titanic concrete structures, but it was just one of many makeshift walkways between the buildings. Higher up the walkways seemed sturdier.

A sudden cold whipped against his face as it found a path between the buildings, and the bridge swayed in its wake. The idea of walking across it filled him with dread. Below them the two towers vanished into the gloom. The bridge looked like it had been constructed years ago; the rope was mildewed and the wooden planks wet and slippery. Jake's eyes tracked them across the chasm. Every so often a gap showed where one had broken and fallen into the darkness below.

Then he saw what Cora was looking at. It was towards the other end of the bridge, mere metres from the safety of the other side – fresh white splinters showed where a plank had recently split.

Snagged on a jagged end of broken board, hanging taut beneath the bridge was a long, tattered scrap of cloth, and at the end of the cloth, fingers knotted white around its end, was the rat-catcher.

And lying on the bridge, on his front, his fingers wrapped around the wrist of the dangling rat-catcher was a child, desperately trying to pull the man to safety.

The wind blew again and the bridge swung, causing the rat-catcher to release another high-pitched yelp.

'Pull, child, pull! I can't be falling back all that way. I'll never be able to make it back up here. I can't bear to go back down!'

The child struggled to lift the man. As he twisted his body with the effort, his face, likewise twisted with pain, turned to Jake.

It was Arkus!

Cora reached the edge of the bridge and tugged one of the ropes that formed the hand rail. It was loose. She looked at the structure. 'One of the main support ropes must've snapped.'

A gust of wind swept between the towers and the

bridge swung again dangerously, making the rat-catcher cry out once more.

'Mercy! Save me from the Underneath! It's even worse than the Lowers.'

'We've *got* to help him,' said Cora. 'The bridge might not be strong enough for both of us, so I think as the braver of us I should—'

But Jake had already stepped out on to the rope-bridge. It creaked under his weight. He looked back at Cora. 'This is all my fault . . . *I'm* going!'

Slowly he edged across the bridge, scarcely believing what he was doing.

Don't look down.

Don't look down.

Don't . . .

He looked down. Down through a gap in the planks. He could not see the ground, just darkness. His head swam and he paused to compose himself. His fingers tightened on the single remaining handrail as once again the bridge rocked precariously against the breeze.

Cora's voice sounded from behind him. 'Faster, Jake, he's slipping.'

Jake quickened his pace until he stood over the gap in the bridge where Arkus lay, still desperately gripping the rat-catcher's hand. Arkus turned, and his eyes opened with fear.

'The assassin!' he gasped.

For a moment their eyes locked.

'I don't care if you do kill me. I'm not going to let go of this poor man's hand.'

Jake blinked. It hadn't occurred to him that this might be the opportune time to carry out his mission. All he saw was a kid, just like himself – albeit with ossicones – trying to save somebody from falling to the Underneath – wherever that was. He knelt by Arkus and, reaching through the broken planks, Jake grabbed the rat-catcher's filthy tunic and started to pull.

For a second the man hung there, not moving, neither Jake nor Arkus speaking, both grimly fixed on the task in hand. Jake's muscles burnt with the effort. For a moment he felt himself starting to slip, and cried out – half with pain, half with the realisation that he could no longer hold on.

Arkus glanced up at him through his spectacles.

'Save yourself, Wormling. The fall won't kill me, I'm invincible.'

The rat-catcher stared up at him with wide, terror-filled eyes.

'Don't you let me go, boy. I won't ever forgive it. I can't go back down there. It ain't nice in these parts but it sure is nicer than the Underneath!'

Jake gritted his teeth. 'I'm not letting him go . . .' But even as his grip tightened he felt the rat-catcher's tunic slipping from his grasp.

'Hang on, Jake!' It was Cora. She was making her way over the bridge, with Zorro and her hockey stick tucked under one arm.

She swore as her foot split another board, and for a second she clung to the swinging bridge with one hand. Soon, though, she was with them, squeezing past Jake and Arkus, to allow Zorro to leap to the safety of the second tower. Cora knelt and gripped the rat-catcher too. Finally, he began to rise, slowly at first, until his other hand could reach the wooden boards, and he scrambled on to the bridge. Together they heaved him on to the cold wet concrete floor where the three children and the rat-catcher lay in an exhausted heap.

Eventually the rat-catcher sat up.

He pulled a face. 'A week's catch. All because of a broken rope.' He peered down into the darkness. 'It happens. Will take a while until someone fixes it. The Authorities don't care much about the lower levels.'

Arkus cleared his throat. 'Actually, that's not strictly true . . .'

The rat-catcher looked him up and down. 'Best you mind your manners when you're talking to one of the dead. You ain't in one of your demon swamp towns now, you know.'

Cora glared up at the rat-catcher. 'Aren't you going to thank us?'

The rat-catcher sneered, revealing brown stumps for teeth. 'Thank you four? A demon, a pair of demon-friends, and a vermin?' He scowled at Arkus. 'If it weren't for his kind in the Authorities, they'd spend some time fixing the bridges for those of us that once trod the Earthly Plane.'

He stood up and started walking away. 'I don't owe demonkind anything, least of all a thank you. Would have been better if he'd've fallen, if you ask me.' He turned and fixed Cora with a stare. 'Would've been one less demon to worry about!' He stalked off.

Cora shook her head at the disappearing rat-catcher.

'What a horrible man.'

Arkus stood up, brushed himself down and shook the dust from the remains of his yellow cloak.

'It's not that poor man's fault he's lost faith in the Afterworld Authorities. He's right that more effort should be spent bettering the lower reaches of Deadhaven . . . But it isn't my father preventing that. He's worked tirelessly to help the dead that live in these parts.'

He removed his spectacles and cleaned them on his suit jacket. Then, putting them back on, he squinted at Jake. 'If you two are supposed to be assassinating me then I'm afraid you're doing a very bad job of it.'

Jake let out a laugh. 'I guess so.'

Cora shook her head. 'It's Jake's destiny not mine.' She nudged him. 'Well done, Jake. You've just managed to save the life of the one demon you're supposed to assassinate.'

Arkus looked up at Cora. 'Actually, I'm invincible. I wouldn't have died if I'd fallen. It would have been very inconvenient, though. The only thing that can kill me is a reaper, and the only reaper who isn't loyal to my father was thankfully destroyed.' He blushed and stared at the floor. 'Hence I'm invincible.'

Jake and Cora exchanged glances.

Invincible apart from the thin, flint dagger hidden in Jake's bag – the flint dagger with the tooth of that very same reaper embedded in its blade. It was ever-present in Jake's mind, a guilty secret only he and Cora knew about. His fingers crept to the bag to check it was still there. Cora frowned at him, and he contented himself by shaking the rucksack and feeling the satisfying weight of it.

For a moment the three children looked at each other. It was Cora who broke the silence. 'Well. This is awkward.'

Jake cleared his throat. 'I wasn't going to assassinate anybody. It's all a misunderstanding.'

Cora shrugged. 'Basically, the Chosen One doesn't want to fulfil his destiny.'

Arkus smiled and waved a hand casually in the

air. 'That's something, at least. I know that feeling well. The weight of *my* calling rests heavy upon these shoulders. It's not easy having to hold the demon nation together. Especially in these troubled times . . . Behold the mark of our enemy . . .'

He pointed to a wall behind them. Crudely scratched in chalk over wet concrete were the words 'Death to all demons'. Below the words a symbol had been drawn, a jagged M, one of its peaks far taller than the other.

He shook his head sadly. 'Even with Fenris thankfully vanquished, not all is peaceful here in Afterworld. These levels of Deadhaven brew rancour.'

'Rancour means bitterness,' whispered Cora to Jake.

'I'd worked that out,' Jake hissed back. He hadn't. His mind was beginning to wander. There was something about the words *death to all demons* . . . Something about the mark, the jagged M. He couldn't quite place it . . .

The small demon smiled sadly. 'Just as Fenris wanted to wipe the dead from the Afterworld, so do a number of the dead want to rid the Afterworld of demons and celestial beings too.'

Jake's mind snapped back to the present. The words of the rat-catcher, at least, were fresh in his mind.

Just a demon.

Jake looked at the floor, embarrassed that a fellow human could dismiss the life of a living creature so easily.

Cora lifted her hat and scratched her head thoughtfully. 'So you don't want to rid the Afterworld of the dead? *You* aren't a follower of Fenris?'

The prince blinked through his spectacles. 'Of course not! My family has dedicated itself to maintaining peace between the occupants of the Afterworld. As king of demons, my father sits alongside the elected rulers of the dead in the Afterworld Authorities.' He seemed sad. 'My father's deathtime draws ever closer.' He took a deep breath. 'When he dies, I will take his place. I hope I am able to rule as justly as he. We're all here for eternity, after all. It makes no sense to fight.'

Jake looked at Cora. 'Then Tokelo Fortune was mistaken . . . Arkus isn't a follower of Fenris!'

The prince frowned. 'Tokelo Fortune thinks that? He's a good friend of my father. Indeed, as Minister of Security, he sits with him as one of he rulers of the Afterworld.' Arkus began to pace back and forth. 'But how would he get that idea? Someone must be spreading false information. Someone who wants me dead. Someone who wants to rid the Afterworld Authorities of their sole demon voice.' He stared at Jake in horror. 'Why, it would plunge the Afterworld into war! Already tension simmers . . .'

Cora brandished her hockey stick. 'They must be stopped! We can't let them kill you.'

Outside the doorway, Jake could see the many towers that made Deadhaven. Beyond those epic towers the Afterworld faded into the distance. Somewhere out there, the battle had taken place between his ancestor Uthred Dragon and Fenris. Fenris had been defeated. The dead could live in peace with demons.

He removed his rucksack and opened it to check

the dagger was still there. It was. He reached in to make sure it was secure, grabbing its handle.

But there would always be tension between the dead and demons. Hadn't the rat-catcher shown that? Maybe it was better that it was ended once and for all? Uthred hadn't stopped at peace. He'd declared war on all demons, seeking to wipe them out, until finally meeting his match with the Hangman of the Void.

Perhaps it was time he continued Uthred's work. Perhaps it *was* time that the Afterworld was rid of demons for good.

Death to demons . . .

'Jake?'

He felt his fingers unwrap from the hilt of the dagger.

It was Cora. She had her hands on his shoulders and was shaking him. 'You went weird and starting muttering to yourself.'

Jake swallowed hard. 'We should get rid of this dagger. It has some strange power over me.'

Arkus looked at him. 'Dagger?'

Jake stared at the floor. 'It was given to me. To

use to destroy you. To send you into the Void.'

Arkus put a hand on Jake's shoulder. 'A dagger cannot harm me.'

Jake looked back at him. 'This one has the tooth of Fenris embedded in its blade.'

Arkus fell silent. 'Maybe I am not as invincible as I thought . . .'

Cora nodded. 'We should throw it from the tower.'

Arkus ran a hand through his hair. 'Throwing it from the building won't destroy the dagger. The thing is, and I hate to be a burden, but as it's the only thing in either world that can send me to the Void, I'd feel better knowing where it is. Does that make sense?'

He looked at Jake shyly. 'You risked your life to save mine – well, you *thought* I was going to die, anyway. I trust you. Do *you* trust that I am not a follower of Fenris?' He reached an open hand towards Jake.

Jake thought of the child who had risked his safety to save the rat-catcher. He reached out and shook the prince's hand. 'I trust you.'

Arkus sighed with relief. 'We need the help of the Afterworld Authorities. We can explain everything.

They will be searching for me. We can just wait here until we're found and then we can get to the bottom of this plot.'

'We might have to be a bit more proactive than that,' Jake said, turning the cloakroom ticket towards Cora. 'It's on 80. It's *still* ticking down. If I'm out of my body for much longer it will die and we'll be trapped here.'

Arkus scratched his left ossicone thoughtfully. 'I know this area. The lower levels of Deadhaven are an unfortunate place – especially for those dead who are unable to work their way upwards. There's a place here. An outpost for the Ministry of Security. If we can find it we can turn ourselves in and get you sent back to the Embassy.'

Jake looked around the dingy surroundings. He glanced at the knife on the floor. Part of him wanted to leave it there, but another part wanted it back safely in his bag. He lowered his rucksack to the floor and pushed the dagger in with his foot. 'I'm not touching it again,' he said, but in his heart he knew this was a lie.

A Plan is Formulated

C ora stopped running. 'Why can't you take us back? Like how you got us here: through the floor.'

Arkus paused at a closed door. He pulled on the handle. It was stuck. 'I can't just do that.' He looked a little cross. 'Not yet anyway. How we got here was by a panic reflex we royal demons have honed to travel to and from the Earthly Plane and the Afterworld whenever we require. I just haven't quite learnt to control it yet.'

Cora chuckled grimly. 'So it takes you to a random place whenever you panic?'

Arkus smiled. 'Almost, but not quite. It's usually a place I have some sort of connection to. An emotional connection. It's hard to describe.' He pointed to the door handle. 'Jake, would you mind?'

Cora looked the smartly dressed demon child up and down. She wiped a finger along the damp wall and held up a fingertip smudged with filth. 'You, a royal demon, have a deep emotional connection with this place?'

Arkus nodded. 'Yes, my father brings me here sometimes. To show what happens when the Authorities don't support those dead who need it most.'

Jake stopped pulling on the handle. 'It won't budge.' He noticed that Arkus suddenly looked sad. 'He sounds like a good man, your dad . . . I mean, he sounds like a good demon.'

Arkus nodded. 'I only hope I can live up to his example. Sometimes it's hard to live up to expectations.'

'Yes,' said Jake.

Cora laughed and reached for the door. 'You'd think – what with both your prestigious ancestors – one of you would know how to open a door.' She wiped a hand over a particularly grubby part of the door, revealing the word 'PUSH', turned the handle and pushed the door open.

DOWN MARKET

The sounds and smells hit Jake like a car. Shouting, swearing voices, people surging past the doorway they'd opened. It was like the corridors at school between lessons except with the occupants of the afterlife instead of school children.

Arkus scratched his head. 'I *think* this is the Down Market,' he said dubiously, 'where the inhabitants of the Lowers gather to buy and swap the wares they've scavenged. The outpost is just at the other end. A few hundred metres to the left . . .' There was a pause. 'At least I think it's the left . . .'

Cora scratched her nose and looked at Arkus. 'Stick with me, your Highness. I don't want to be spending the rest of my deathtime trying to find you in a crowd.'

She turned to Jake. 'You take Zorro. We don't want to lose him.'

Jake smiled. 'And what if *I* get lost?'

Cora shrugged. 'Your ticket's almost run out anyway. When it gets to zero you'll be trapped here whatever!' She took Arkus by the hand. 'We'll get you to the outpost safely. Then we need to get back home as soon as possible and clear this mess up.'

Jake picked up Zorro and tucked him underneath his arm, taking the opportunity to stroke his head, something he couldn't do in the Earthly Plane on account of Zorro having no physical presence there. Cora pushed out into the crowd and immediately disappeared amongst the hordes of people rushing past.

Taking a deep breath, Jake too pushed out into the throng. The Down Market was actually just a long corridor, similar to but wider than the one they had fallen into upon their arrival. This corridor was lined with tiny stalls, and was full of people, tightly packed together, all forcing their way through the scrum.

For a second the crowd parted slightly and Jake

glimpsed a flash of Cora. He pushed his way through, apologising as he went – eventually catching up with her and Arkus.

'There are so many people,' she said.

He nodded and looked around. The market was rammed full of people of every shape and place and era – people who had once walked upon the Earthly Plane as living beings, now fully paid-up members of the dead.

'Do they live here?' he asked Arkus.

Arkus nodded. 'Mainly. Some are passing through, though. The dead who happen to have arrived at the bottom of the towers and are working their way upwards. There are celestial folk as well.' He pointed to a scaly winged creature sitting on a beam that ran high across the corridor. Here and there were animals too. A dog lay asleep beneath a table loaded with ragged sheets and carpets. And there were rats. Lots of rats.

Jake felt something tugging at his trouser leg. He looked down and was surprised to see a small, grey, gargoyle-like creature grabbing at his jeans with clawed fingers.

'You buying?' it rasped. It gazed up at him with large round eyes in its squished face and raised an arm to reveal a selection of what looked like ancient electrical devices hanging from the leathery webbing beneath his arm. 'Calculators. Very, very good.'

Jake shook his head, and the gargoyle opened its other wing to reveal a selection of mobile phones that were even older than Jake's dad's.

'Tellyphones cheap here,' it added, some dribble escaping from its mouth and dripping down its chin.

'No thank you.' Jake pulled his trouser leg free of the creature's grasp, and pushed through the crowd after Cora once more. He couldn't see her now. The wide corridor was lined with metal shutters. Most of them were open, revealing alcoves that housed tiny shops where both humans and strange celestial creatures sold all manner of things. Nearby was the shop that Jake assumed might have been the end destination for the rat-catcher's produce. Bunches of rats hung from the back wall, and behind the counter, a young woman rotated several skewered ones over a charcoal grill.

Once again Jake felt the gargoyle's claws on his jeans.

'What you want here?' it asked. 'You not from the Lowers . . . Snelf can help guide you back upstairs. Or help you buy crab apple real cheap.'

It jerked Jake towards a stall selling strange fruit. Beneath the table wicker baskets were filled with tiny, sour-looking apples.

'I'm sorry,' said Jake firmly, pulling himself free once more. 'I need to find my . . .'

His voice was drowned out by the sudden sound of angry shouting.

The gargoyle's eyes opened wide with fright, and it froze, dead still, its skin changing from grey to green, perfectly matching the crab apples it stood beside.

Jake paused. 'Are you OK?'

The demon spoke through closed lips. 'Bad dead. Not fond of gargoyle. Not liking demonkind!' it hissed. 'Go. Leave Snelf.'

Jake looked up in horror. The shouting came from the direction in which Cora and Arkus had disappeared.

Hadn't the chalk writing said 'Death to Demons'?
Arkus might be in trouble.

Taking a deep breath, Jake pushed his way through the crowd in the direction of the shouting.

THE OUTPOST

'You should be ashamed of yourself, picking on a child!'

Jake heard Cora's voice before he saw her. The crowd had drawn back from her and a tall man who was holding on to Arkus's arm.

Cora was circling menacingly, gripping her hockey stick.

This time Arkus didn't look panicked. If anything he seemed angry. He pulled against the man's grip. 'You don't understand what you're doing.'

The man held on tightly. He was stripped to the waist, and Jake recognised the mark of the jagged M crudely tattooed across his chest. The same mark they'd seen on the wall. It was the mark of those who wanted the extermination of all demons.

Jake swallowed nervously.

'This market is for the dead only. We don't want you demons here stealing our things!' said the man.

A woman's voice called from the crowd. 'Shame on you, Derek! There have been demons here since long before you scuttled in from the Earthly Plane!'

There was laughter from the crowd. It was obvious not everyone agreed with the man.

He glared back at them. 'Those that think demonkind can be trusted are traitors,' he spat. He grabbed a fistful of Arkus's cloak, lifting the child on to his tiptoes. 'This fine cloth. Where did you get it? Stolen, no doubt.'

Cora stepped forward. 'It's none of your business. Let him go.'

The big man laughed. 'Or what, Princess? And who put you in charge?'

Arkus looked up at the man. 'Actually, my father is—'

The man spoke over him, and started to push his way through the gathered crowd. 'No demons in the market.' He was dragging Arkus across the floor. 'I'll throw you out myself. All the way to the Underneath.'

Jake took a step forward, hardly believing he was actually doing it. He blocked the man's path. 'You're hurting him!' he shouted. 'Let him go.'

There was a murmur of approval from the masses. The lady's voice rang out again. 'Shame on you, Derek. You listen to the lad. He's got more good in his little finger than you have in your whole body.'

The man looked around uneasily. He wasn't used to being challenged. Least of all by another child. To be honest, Jake hadn't been expecting to challenge him either. The guy was massive.

He leant down and pressed his face close to Jake's. 'Get out of my way, traitor,' he hissed, flecks of spit hitting Jake's eyes.

Another voice spoke from the crowd. 'Calm yourself, Derek, the skulls will be here soon. Best you put the demon lad down so we can all get on with our business.'

'I'm not scared of the Authorities,' the man named Derek retorted. 'The Down Market belongs to the dead!' He went to push Jake out of his way, but something caught between his feet and he stumbled forward.

Once again Jake found himself in a tangle of bodies – himself, Arkus and this giant of a man. Cora stood over them.

'The bigger they come,' she said, unhooking her hockey stick from the man's ankle.

The crowd laughed again.

'She got you there, Derek! Knocked over by a princess.'

The man scowled and clambered back to his feet, looking embarrassed. Jake followed suit, pulling Arkus up to stand.

Cora winked at Jake. 'Any other time you need some help, just let me know.'

The man turned to Jake, keen to take out his embarrassment on somebody. 'What are you smiling at? You little traitor.' He grabbed Jake by the collar of his hoodie and lifted him from the ground. Jake stared down at the two huge hands: tattooed knuckles reading 'HATE' on one hand. He looked across at the other fist. Those knuckles read 'HATE' too.

Jake looked up. 'I'm not scared of bullies like you,' he said, his voice cracking with fear.

A strange look passed over the man's face. First

it went red, a boiling rage. Then he paled, like the blood had drained from it. He let go of Jake's collar. 'Just having some fun with you . . .' He stepped backwards into the crowd.

Jake sighed with relief. It was amazing. Apparently if you stood up to a bully they backed down. That's what people said. And it really worked. He winked at Cora, saying, 'Not so helpless after all . . .'

Her face made him stop. She was staring over his shoulder. In fact, the whole crowd had fallen silent. They were all looking behind him.

Jake slowly turned around.

The face of a skeleton loomed back at him.

'Jake Green, you are under arrest for the attempted assassination of Prince Arkus the Invincible! I'm licensed by the Authorities to place you under the touch of Rigor Mortis.' The terrifying figure reached out and touched Jake's shoulder with a single bony finger. Jake felt his body stiffen, then fall. As the light dimmed in his eyes, the last thing he saw was the small gargoyle scuttling off to safety between the legs of the crowd.

PERSONA NON GRATA

Jake opened his eyes at the sound of scraping metal. He was in a small cell in complete darkness apart from a shaft of light that shone in from a tiny square hatch. It was the hatch screeching open that had woken him.

A feeling of dread surged through his body.

'How long have I been asleep?' he blurted out, digging for the cloakroom ticket in his pocket. If it read zero it would mean that his body had died on the Earthly Plane.

The ticket was gone.

And so was his rucksack. Which meant that the dagger and tooth were gone too.

Jake started scrabbling around the floor, looking for his bag, hoping that someone had thrown it in the cell with him, that it was somewhere there, hidden in the shadows.

He stopped at the sound of the door opening, then shielded his eyes from the bright light suddenly flooding the room.

'Your belongings are safe, Jake,' said a familiar voice, 'but you are in danger. You must come this way.'

Jake blinked, his eyes adjusting to the new light. 'I know you,' he said. 'You're the demonologist. You were wrong about Prince Arkus.'

The demonologist looked around nervously. 'Yes. Cora has already informed me of our little misunderstanding. She's safe, by the way, so is Arkus. For the moment. But I'm afraid – due to you being caught with the knife – you're very much *persona non grata* in the Afterworld.'

'*Persona non grata?* Does that mean something bad?'

'Something bad is an understatement of your current predicament, Jake.'

'Can't we explain to the Authorities that—'

The demonologist nodded. 'Of course . . . of course. That's what we're going to do. This way. And quickly.' He led Jake from the cell and into a corridor. 'But until then, every demon, skeleton, gargoyle and celestial creature of any kind wants your head on a plate. We need to get you to safety.'

He paused at the sound of footsteps approaching, then put a hand on Jake's shoulder and guided him into an empty cell as a skeleton guard walked past.

'This is a delicate situation,' he explained in an undertone once the guard had passed. 'Everything must be handled correctly. We've summoned Major Stiffkey as Cora asked. I'm taking you to him now.'

The sound of Stiffkey's name made Jake feel immediately better. Stiffkey would sort it out. Once he'd been an undertaker, then the ghost of an undertaker. Now, however, he was a senior commander in the security forces.

The demonologist checked the skeleton guard was safely out of sight.

'Just down here,' he said, leading Jake down the darkened corridor to a door. 'Stiffkey will be with us any minute. But until then it's best we operate on a need-to-know basis.' He tapped his nose conspiratorially. 'The skeletons in the security forces represent demonkind. If they found out that the accused assassin was here, we might not be able to let you go as easily, even with Prince Arkus's blessing.'

Jake nodded.

'And besides, there's someone else here, incognito. Someone you need to talk to . . . But first, your belongings.' He opened one of the lockers that lined the corridor and took out Jake's cloakroom ticket.

48

Jake let out a sigh of relief. Sure, it wasn't long to get back to the Earthly Plane. But at least he hadn't been unconscious too long. And at least his body was still alive.

'The paralysis touch only lasted a few minutes. You still have enough time for Stiffkey to get you back.' The demonologist smiled reassuringly, then reached into the locker again, before handing Jake his rucksack. 'This is yours, I believe.' He smiled again, as Jake gratefully took it.

He unzipped it. Firstly he checked for Cora's trophy. It was still there. Safe. So was something else.

'The knife! It's still in there. But I don't need it any more.'

The demonologist nodded. 'Yes, Jake, you do.'

Jake tried to give him the rucksack back. 'I don't want to touch it. You take it out. Can't you keep it until Stiffkey gets here?' Even as he spoke, the fingers of his left hand started to work their way towards the handle.

The demonologist opened a door. Something had changed in his face. He seemed less nervous. He was smiling. 'Why don't you hold the dagger one last time, Jake?'

Jake didn't want to but before he knew what he was doing, his fingers had closed around the hilt. The stone handle fitted perfectly in his hand.

'It feels good, doesn't it, Jake? Powerful.'

Jake drew the blade from the rucksack. He felt strong. It was good to see the tooth again. 'When's Stiffkey getting here again?' he asked distractedly, his eyes beginning to glaze over.

He shook his head to clear his clouded mind.

The jagged shape of the blade echoed the crooked M symbol he'd seen scrawled on the wall outside.

Death to demons.

Suddenly, something else clicked in Jake's head. A memory of where else he'd seen that mark. The jagged M, tattooed on the wrist of the demonologist.

Everything became clear.

'I know who told Tokelo Fortune the lie that Arkus was a follower of Fenris . . . I know who has tricked him into thinking Arkus must be assassinated! That mark. It's the same shape as the dagger – the only weapon that can send Arkus to the Void. The weapon that belongs to the Chosen One.'

He looked up at the demonologist in horror. 'It was you!'

The demonologist looked at Jake mockingly. 'Please continue . . .'

'If you're a demon-hater then it would explain all of this. You must've been waiting all this time for the tooth to be found so you could get rid of the prince of demons. Didn't Tokelo say there was no other heir?'

Jake felt weak. He stumbled forward against the door.

The demonologist reached out to him. He took

Jake by the shoulder and guided him through into the room. 'You cannot escape your destiny, Jake. The tooth will send the prince to the Void but it is the stone blade that compels the Chosen One to act on the prophecy. Its power is far greater in the Afterworld than in the Embassy of the Dead. This time you will not be able to resist . . .'

DESTINY CALLING

'Jake!'

Jake blinked. He was walking, walking towards a table. Something was on the table. Something that writhed and twisted, a being held by a strange rope looped many times around the table. It was Arkus. But it wasn't Arkus who had called his name. It was Cora.

'Jake!'

Jake turned his head towards where the voice was coming from. He tried to speak but no sound came from his mouth.

The rope that bound Arkus to the table trailed to where Cora sat. Whoever had tied Arkus to the table had used the same thing to strap her to the chair. Jake could see now that it wasn't a rope, but a strange vine that branched in twists and turns

185

around both Arkus and Cora.

'Jake! For goodness sake. Snap out of it!'

He blinked. Cora again. A gag had been around her mouth, but she'd managed to work it free somehow. She was still calling to him. 'Don't do it, Jake!'

Do what? Was he still dreaming?

He took another step towards the table.

'Don't do what?' he mumbled to himself. He looked at the demon prince and his hand went to the vine. 'Why are you tied—?'

'It's that Enchanted Deathweed stuff!' shouted Cora. 'It's stopping his panic reflex!'

Deathweed. The plant that neutralised demon magic.

Jake gazed down at his left hand and was surprised to discover that he was holding the dagger. He began to lift the dagger into the air.

Beyond Jake's view of the dagger, Arkus struggled against the Enchanted Deathweed. He looked like he was starting to panic, struggling for breath, jerking against the thick vine that prevented him slipping away to safety.

Cora too was struggling against the vine. 'You'll never get away with this,' she shouted at the Demonolgoist. 'When Tokelo Fortune finds out how you've tricked him—'

A voice sounded from the other side of the room. 'Your faith in my loyalty to the Authorities is touching, Ms Sanderford. I'm afraid I've long since lost confidence in their ability to rule the Afterworld.'

An image of a doorway was starting to appear in the wall – the same apparition that they'd seen only that morning in the demonologist's bookshop. Tokelo Fortune leant against the doorframe, his head tucked beneath his arm.

'I apologise I can't be there in person.' He smiled. 'But I did want to make sure everything was finished to my specifications.'

The demonologist turned to Tokelo, bowing slightly. 'Everything is ready. This time the power of the stone dagger will be too strong for the Wormling. Nothing can stop us now.'

Once more Jake tried to unwrap his fingers from the dagger. But once more his hand refused to respond.

Tokelo smiled again. 'And nobody is aware of your presence in the security forces outpost?'

'Nobody,' replied the demonologist. 'Nothing links the assassination back to you. You will still be trusted by the Authorities and the ensuing troubles will ensure increased powers for the Minister of Security.'

'Silence!' spat back Tokelo. 'Your careless chatter is unnecessary. I am aware of my own success. The details of our plot should not be spoken aloud.'

The demonologist winced. 'Yes, Minister. Only those in this room know of our plot,' he said. 'And as you can see, you and I will be the only witnesses to their being sent to the Eternal Void.'

A large grin spread across Tokelo's face. 'You and I is one person too many.' He chuckled.

A look of fear flashed across the demonologist's face. 'I don't understand. My loyalty to the cause is—'

The words died on his lips. He froze suddenly, his eyes opening wide in an expression of pain and shock. 'I am betrayed,' he whispered.

Jake could see something happening to the demonologist's face. It was withering, greying – as if he was ageing before them, his eyes dulled, the skin first pulled tight and dry around his skull, then ripped like paper to reveal powdering flesh. He dropped to the floor.

'It is coming for you,' he croaked. He stayed like that for a second – teetering on his knees before toppling, falling flat on his face in a cloud of dust that slowly settled on the floor, the only evidence that he had ever existed at all.

Something moved amidst the dust: a large, spider-like creature.

'The Gomseer!' breathed Cora.

Its bite will paralyse then desiccate the living or the dead.

Tokelo spoke. 'We cannot escape our destinies, Wormling. Your connection to the demon-slayer Uthred Dragon is too strong. It is important that the prophecy is fulfilled willingly. Give yourself to the stone dagger.'

Jake tried to shout but he couldn't. Instead he took another step forward. He stood over the struggling, chained demon prince, the power of the flint blade coursing through his body.

The prince was now convulsing uncontrollably, the vine that bound him and prevented his panic reflex digging into his demon flesh. Jake could see that he was crying, and he could feel tears forming in his own eyes.

His fingers tightened their grip on the dagger. Still higher he raised the knife.

'It is my destiny,' he murmured. But the voice was not his own. They felt like the words of someone else.

A shadow moved in the darkness and for a moment Jake's head cleared. It was Zorro slinking from the corner of the room, looking for his owner. Jake followed him with his eyes as he hopped on to Cora's lap, seemingly oblivious to the situation.

'It is your time.'

Jake nodded grimly. It was his time. He lifted the dagger above his head and spoke. 'It is my destiny.'

It was not his will. But it was his destiny. And who was he – a mere child – to question an ancient prophecy? Hadn't he seen it unfold in his vision? Wasn't his future already written?

Or was it?

In the vision the prince had not been bound. There

had been a broken model boat. This was different. For a moment Jake's eyes met the frightened eyes of Arkus, straining against the Deathweed and he felt the fear that was coursing through both their bodies.

The call of the dagger was strong.

But not strong enough.

Jake wrapped his fingers even tighter around the hilt of the dagger. He took a deep breath and plunged it downwards, striking the vine to the side of Arkus, severing it in two and leaving the dagger embedded in the table. Arkus looked up at Jake.

'You . . . you did not send me to the Void.'

Jake yanked the dagger from the table. 'I may be the Chosen One but this is not the chosen time.'

Arkus stared. He reached out for Jake's hand, and Jake took his. 'Thank you, friend,' said the demon prince, sinking into the floor again, severed vines and all, pulling Jake after him.

Cora watched Jake and the prince disappear through the floor. 'Great!' she muttered sarcastically. She looked at Tokelo Fortune. 'The prince got away, though.'

A flash of annoyance crossed Tokelo's face, only to be replaced by a cruel grin. 'It seems I've underestimated the Wormling's power to resist the will of the stone dagger,' he said. 'But what to do with you, Ms Sanderford? You're an interesting case, for sure. A dead mother and father . . .' He paused, smiling at the look of shock on Cora's face. 'Oh. You didn't realise that your father is dead too now. Rest assured, he's as unpopular in death as he was in life.'

Cora swallowed, as Tokelo continued. 'You never got to say goodbye. You never got to make your peace and say sorry.'

Cora shook her head angrily. 'It wasn't me who needed to apologise. It was him.'

Tokelo clicked his fingers and there was a movement in the shadows. It was the Gomseer. 'You needed to apologise for not living up to his expectations. Your life was a failure. And now it's too late. If you weren't about to be drained by my beautiful pet then you'd be impossible to Undo. It would be hundreds of years before you joined your loved ones.'

The Gomseer tensed on the floor before them, readying itself to pounce.

'My father never loved me anyway,' shouted Cora, her rage bringing burning tears to her eyes. 'He was more concerned with his studies, his history, his precious ancestry!'

Tokelo froze. A strange look passed across his face.

Cora felt the chair move slightly.

Zorro shifted in her lap but Cora held him tight. Despite her predicament – alone in the Afterlife, bound in a chair, facing the mandibles of a Gomseer – Cora smiled. The vine that had bound her to the prince had tightened – the same vine that led to the slowly disappearing hole in the floor. Now – as the prince and Jake began their fall to another world – they finally pulled taut and began to pull at her chair. It began to slide along the floor, at first slowly then speeding up towards the hole.

The Gomseer leapt. Zorro's jaw flashed and he caught the spider-creature and flung it sideways. It landed on its feet and immediately started scuttling towards them once more. The vine pulled tighter and the chair toppled as it sped towards the closing hole, pulling Cora and Zorro with it. For a split second the chair and the tethered girl teetered on the edge of the hole, and as it continued to close it seemed that they might not make it in time. But with a jerk and a twist, Cora toppled down the hole after Arkus and Jake.

The last thing Cora saw as she left the Lowers of Deadhaven was the face of Tokelo Fortune. His face still wore a strange expression, and as she fell Cora realised what it was.

He looked pleased.

BACK TO EARTH WITH A BUMP

J ake groaned and his groan was answered with
another.

'Prince Arkus?' he whispered. 'Are you OK?'

'I think so,' came the prince's voice from the
darkness, close by. 'Thank you, Jake.'

Jake sat up. 'Thank you for what? I nearly killed
you.'

'But you didn't,' replied Arkus. 'You fought
against the power of the dagger. You made your own
destiny. A new destiny. A destiny that unites the
Afterworld in peace, instead of locking it into an
everlasting war.'

Jake sat in silence for a moment, glad of the pitch
black. Sometimes he found it hard to take a
compliment.

'So where are we?' asked Arkus.

Jake's eyes slowly adjusted to the gloom. He was sitting on the floor of his bedroom at his mum's house.

'We're home,' he said, dragging himself to his feet and turning on the bedside light beneath the window. 'Well . . . I'm home, I mean. This is my house.'

The prince blinked in the sudden brightness. Then he looked around Jake's bedroom, taking in the messy desk, the pile of dirty laundry and the random stuff scattered everywhere. 'You live in the slums of Deadhaven?'

Jake frowned. 'This is the Earthly Plane. This is my bedroom.'

The prince blushed. 'I do apologise.'

To be fair to the demon prince, it was a little untidy. Jake scratched his head.

'I don't understand. How did we get here? You're supposed to have some sort of connection to the place you fall to, right? This is my bedroom!'

Arkus shook his head. 'With each fall I grow weaker. My panic reflex uses a lot of energy. As I grow weaker, your influence in the fall grows stronger.'

He paled.

'I may not have the energy for another fall.'

Jake looked down at himself. He was semi-transparent. 'I'm still a ghost!' he said, stating the obvious. He reached out to the window and pressed his hand against the pane, taking a breath as he felt the cold evening air through the glass.

It was the first time he'd tested his presence in the Earthly Plane. Bar a few seconds in the kitchen, the only time he'd been out of his body was either in the Embassy of the Dead or the Afterworld.

'I've got a physical presence.'

He began to unwind the Deathweed vine that was still partially wrapped around Arkus's chest.

The window felt strange, though, almost as though his hand was slightly numb. All ghosts were different. Some of them had a certain solidity, an ability to move objects, others had no physical presence, like Cora - she couldn't affect the objects around her, apart from with her hockey stick. On the other hand, she could walk through walls. It had come in handy a couple of times. Other times, like when Jake was trying to go to the toilet - not so much. She was annoying like that, Cora.

Cora!

She'd been left behind with Fortune and the Gomseer.

'Cora! We've left her—'

He jumped at the sound of someone clearing their throat.

'Thought you'd got rid of me?'

His eyes followed the vine across his bedroom floor, over his bed and off the other side into the small space between it and the wall. A familiar pair of smart school shoes stuck up from the gap.

It was Cora. He leant over the bed. She was still wrapped in the enchanted vines. At her feet was Zorro. Even he was looking at Jake slightly reproachfully.

Cora's eyes narrowed. 'Lucky the demonologist had tied me to the prince. I was dragged through the hole after you.'

Jake scratched his nose nervously. 'All part of my elaborate escape plan,' he lied.

Cora looked him up and down. 'You're awfully shimmery, Jake.'

Jake inspected his hand again. It was weird being

able to see through a part of his own body. 'I am, aren't I?' Jake took the cloakroom ticket from his pocket. *33.* He showed it to Cora.

'Probably time to get your body back from Eustace before it dies,' said Cora breezily, but Jake could see her concern matched his own.

He sighed with relief as he remembered where Eustace was. 'He's downstairs waiting for us!'

The thought of seeing Eustace again was reassuring to Jake. At the very least he could go back to being a normal boy. Well, as close to a normal boy as the heir to Uthred Dragon, demon-slayer, could ever be. Jake paused at the top of the stairs at the familiar sound of Sab's laughter, and the weirder one of his own voice saying, 'Dear Sab! You really are a card!'

It was Eustace-in-his-body.

'At least *they're* having fun,' he said to Cora, following Zorro down the stairs and watching the fox scamper through into the kitchen.

'Ooh, you've got post!' said Cora.

Jake stooped to pick up a parcel. It was marked with the logo of the Embassy of the Dead. He jammed the package into his rucksack.

Jake stopped in the hallway as Zorro came running out again with his tail between his legs. He scratched where the fox's ears would have been if they'd had any physical existence. 'What's up, Zorro?' he asked.

He looked up at Cora in horror as he heard the sound of his mum laughing.

'Mum's back!' he hissed.

He crept to the kitchen door and peered around the corner.

His mum, Sab and Eustace-in-his-body were sitting around the table, halfway through a conversation.

'And so you're doing Latin now?' asked his mum incredulously.

Jake's heart caught in his throat. His eyes flicked to Sab who had his head in his hands.

'Of course, Mother!' replied Eustace-in-Jake's-body.

Jake's mum raised her eyebrows. 'Isn't it a dead language?'

Eustace-in-Jake's-body smiled back politely. '*Condemnant quod non intellegunt.* They condemn that which they do not understand.'

If Jake's mum's eyebrows could rise any higher they would have.

Eustace-in-Jake's-body continued unabashed. 'Latin is the father of the Romance languages, Mother. French, English, Italian . . .'

Jake's mum sighed, then turned to Sab. 'So you're staying over tonight, Sab? Have you checked with your mum?'

She paused, noting something strange on the table.

'What's the ham doing out?'

Eustace-in-Jake's-body was about to reply when his eyes caught sight of Zorro calmly padding across the kitchen floor.

'What the devil?' he murmured.

'What's that, Jake? Don't mumble, love,' said his mum.

'Nothing, Mother . . . Mum,' Eustace added quickly.

Sab, too, had noticed Zorro. His eyes tracked back in the direction that Zorro had entered from and saw the ghost Jake peering into the kitchen.

Jake motioned upwards. Even though he was a ghost and he knew his mum wasn't going to be able to see him, he couldn't quite bring himself to say, 'Meet me upstairs,' just in case she had suddenly developed sensitivity to the paranormal. After all, he'd be in real trouble if she found out that not only had he snuck out of his house that evening, but he'd also snuck out of his body, and the Earthly Plane too.

Sab looked at Eustace-in-Jake's-body and nodded to the doorway. Eustace-in-Jake's-body glanced up and saw Jake peering in. He smiled with what could only be described as immense relief.

'Sab, we should go upstairs. Maybe play some . . . whist?'

Jake groaned. Having died in the 1940s, Eustace wasn't too well versed in the pastimes of modern kids to say the least.

His mum frowned again.

'No playing cards online.' She picked up the packet of half-eaten ham and put it back in the fridge. 'Now clear off, so I can make us dinner.'

Jake sighed. It seemed his mum was none the wiser, and for just a second it seemed that everything was going to be OK.

Just a second.

Arkus gasped. Jake turned around to see Cora and Arkus backing away from a huge hooded figure morphing through the front door, the scythe strapped to his back clonking against the light shade. The man's cloak shone with silver starlit threads, embroidered symbols and scenes that seemed to disappear into the distance as if his robes were woven from the fabric of space. The man was so tall he had to stoop to avoid scraping his head, and while his face was hidden in the shadow of the hood, a living beard grew like vines from the darkness.

Around his neck hung a grisly pendant: a dead white hare.

Jake had met this spectral giant before, of course, and to be honest had been hoping he would never have to meet him again.

It was Mawkins: the grimmest of the grim reapers.

Mawkins paused, seeming a little surprised to find Jake standing right in front of him. The hare around his neck twitched slightly, and its dead eyes flicked open.

To the horror of all those in the hallway, the hare

opened its mouth and began to speak in a voice that was not of this world.

'Jake Green, Cora Sanderford, I sentence you both to the Eternal—'

He was interrupted by a squeal from Arkus. Jake turned to see the terrified prince struggling for breath, clutching at his throat, as he had at the Embassy, and again in Deadhaven.

Jake reached out for Arkus. 'He's panicking.'

He looked up at Cora, who stood over the prince.

'I thought he didn't have enough energy to—'

Before he could finish, a hole opened beneath Arkus and once again he fell, Cora and Zorro tumbling after him. Jake stood for a second, staring up at Mawkins. Then he grabbed his rucksack and leapt after them, just as the hole was closing.

GLASS HOUSE

Jake sat up. He was in a large room, lit by moonlight and empty apart from what he assumed to be furniture draped in white sheets, and a whole load of cardboard boxes. One side of the room was walled entirely by glass, and looked over a small pebbled beach leading downwards to a giant body of water, which was ringed by rusty heathland peppered with mossy boulders. On the shore of the lake stood a boat house, suspended on stilts, half over the water. The other way along the pebbly lakefront was a jetty. Next to the jetty, half sunk and barely visible in the night, were the remains of a boat.

Cora, Zorro and Arkus stood gazing from the window.

It was quite a view.

Jake wandered over to his friends. Where was

this? It could be anywhere for all he knew. Anywhere with a massive lake and no other houses as far as the eye could see. He turned to Arkus. 'Where are we? Do you have a connection to this place?'

Arkus shrugged. 'No idea! I thought you might . . .' He looked from the window. 'It's a lovely view,' he said. Then he turned to Jake. 'Are you sure you don't know where we are? Maybe your presence in the fall means the place has a connection to you, like last time?'

Jake looked round the huge room. A roll of bubble wrap lay on the table. He stepped over to one of the white cloths and lifted it gingerly. Underneath was a huge leather sofa. 'Check out the size of that sofa!' he said. He rubbed the back of his head. 'I think whoever lives here is halfway through moving out.' He caught sight of his translucent reflection in the window. 'We're on the Earthly Plane, though, because I'm still a ghost.'

'Maybe it's the house of somebody you know?' said Arkus.

Jake thought about his mum's house and his dad's flat, both of which could fit into the space of this room alone. 'Believe me,' he said, 'no one I know lives in a house like this.' He tilted his head to one side, listening to the silence. He could hear nothing.

'So you don't know *anyone* who would live in a house like this?' said Cora, peering into an open box. She pointed to a faded photo of a young girl of about four years old.

Jake picked it up.

'Still no idea?' she asked.

Jake looked at the photo and shrugged. 'Is it someone famous?'

'Yes,' said Cora, smiling. 'I suppose a bit . . .'

Jake squinted. The girl was dressed in a school uniform and stood next to a suitcase. She was smiling proudly, obviously enjoying being the centre of attention.

'She looks quite spoilt,' said Jake thoughtfully. 'Like she might be a bit bratty . . .'

Cora raised an eyebrow. 'Nothing wrong with a bit of self-confidence.' She side-eyed him. 'It was a big day.'

Jake flipped the photo round and read the handwritten words on the back aloud: 'Cora's first day at St Bodelean's . . .' He paused. 'This is your house!' He looked at the floor. 'Sorry, Cora.'

'No apology needed, Precious,' said Cora breezily. 'It's my father's house and, judging by the packing boxes, the dust, and the fact that my father designed this house and would *never* choose to move out, I can be sure . . .' She gazed out of the window. 'I can be sure Fortune was telling the truth: he's dead.'

Jake swallowed nervously. It seemed wrong to talk like that. He thought again about how he would feel if his dad had died, and he couldn't even imagine it. He looked at her. 'How can you be so sure?'

She pointed to a card on the mantelpiece. The word *Condolences* was written across a watercolour vase of flowers. 'A clue,' she deadpanned.

Jake picked it up. Inside was written: *Yours, Maud.*

'My auntie,' explained Cora. 'Father's older sister. Notice there is just one card. He was very unpopular. It's not addressed to anyone either. He probably died alone.'

Jake rubbed the back of his head. 'It doesn't mean . . .'

'I draw your attention to exhibit B.' She pointed to a leaflet on one of the boxes. An order of service for the funeral of Lord Sanderford, buried at St Joseph's church. It was dated three days ago. 'Plus Tokelo told me. I think he was trying to make me upset. It didn't work.' She took the leaflet from the mantelpiece. 'Not what Father would have wanted – to be buried in a churchyard, I mean. But that's what happens when you leave the world with no friends. There's no one to make sure your final wishes are fulfilled.'

Jake could see her reflection in the window, watching his reaction. He looked at the floor, desperate to escape her glare, yet knowing that whatever he should be doing as a friend, it wasn't looking away. He wished there was something he could say. He cleared his throat, still unable to meet her eye. 'I just want you to know that if you . . .' he began awkwardly.

'Don't bother, Precious,' she said. Her hockey stick materialised in her hand and she used the end to start rummaging in the nearest box. With a skilful twist and flick of her wrists, she picked a hockey ball from the box, balancing it on the flat side of her stick.

'What *would* he have wanted?' asked Jake quietly.

'Eh?' said Cora.

'You said he wouldn't have wanted to be buried in a churchyard.'

She laughed. 'He would have wanted to be entombed in his precious house. Like an Anglo Saxon king!' She motioned around the building. 'Either that or to be pushed out to sea on a burning longboat like a Viking.'

Jake blinked.

'He was a professor of history. Obsessed with his family tree,' she explained. She pointed to a box of books. 'Probably all ones he wrote. He wasn't very interested in other people's lives.' She let the hockey ball fall to the floor. 'Especially if they didn't want to follow in his footsteps.' She put on a deep voice. 'All Sanderfords achieve, Cora. Every generation furthered the Sanderford name, and you must too. Why, I can trace our family back to blah de blah de blah . . .' She looked down at the ball. 'I never really listened. I wanted to play hockey in the Olympics, not study ancient history.'

Jake nodded. 'I see,' he said lamely. 'Maybe he

just wanted the best for you . . .' His words tailed off and he cursed himself for being so stupid. What did he know about Cora's father?

She smiled sympathetically and pointed to the large fireplace. 'When we found out that I was dying, he burnt my hockey stick. I think that's why it came back with my ghost.'

Jake gasped. 'Why? That's crazy!'

Cora shrugged. 'He said all that sport had been a waste of time. He said I could have been learning something important. Something that brought honour to the Sanderford name.' She hugged her hockey stick. 'Not many other ghosts get their own spectral artefacts. That's why I got mine.' She sighed and gestured around. 'Home sweet home. Not that I ever got to stay here . . . I was always at St Bodelean's School for Girls . . .'

There was the sound of a bang from behind them. Jake spun round to see Arkus lying on the floor, his face pale.

Jake rushed to his side. 'Arkus! Are you OK?'

The prince's eyelids flickered open. 'It's all the panicking. Each leap drains my energy,' he whispered.

'Can you get back to the Afterworld somehow? Maybe you'll end up somewhere safe?'

Arkus shook his head. 'Even if I could control my final destination, I have no energy left. I'm stuck here.'

Jake looked at Cora. 'We need to get him to the Embassy as soon as possible –where it's safe.'

Cora nodded.

'And us, too. They've sent out Mawkins. They still think we're assassins, even though we actually saved Arkus.'

She banged her hockey stick on the floor. 'We need to tell them about Tokelo Fortune, too. If only we still had the Mousephone. There must be some other way. Somebody else we can ask for help.'

Jake stared out of the window at the bleak moorland. He shook his head in disbelief. 'Let's face it. It seems like there's nobody at all for miles – let alone anybody who can help us get to the Embassy.' He grimaced at Cora. 'I wish there was somebody here! Somebody who—' He stopped.

There was the unmistakable sound of breaking glass. Someone was in the house.

Jake swallowed.

The phrase 'be careful what you wish for' sprang to mind.

THE BATHROOM

Deciding to get out of the house as quickly as possible had been Jake's idea, unsurprisingly.

'Through the bathroom!' whispered Cora. 'It's on the ground floor, through there. We can get out the window.' She pointed across the huge room to a door.

Jake pulled Arkus's arm over his shoulder and heaved him to his feet. Stumbling across the large room, he reached the door. Gently, he sat the prince on the floor, leaning him against the wall. 'Don't worry. We won't leave you here.'

He stood and pushed the door open. Then he stopped in his tracks. The floor was wet. The bath was overflowing.

Someone was in the tub!

'I'm glad you've joined us, Wormling,' came a woman's voice. 'It's good to meet you properly.'

A fully dressed lady stood up from the water, bone dry. Jake recognised her drab clothing and her large, curved nose. It was one of the twins from the Embassy. Nancy Mittle – the ghost assistant of her sister Agnes.

'You're not wet,' said Jake. It was all he could think of to say.

The ghost of Nancy Mittle smiled. 'I'm a spectre with no physical presence. Water doesn't stick to my clothes. I have no form.' She giggled and stepped through the side of the bath, as if to illustrate the point. 'I was just reminiscing!' She looked at Cora, who was standing in the doorway. 'You understand, don't you, darling? I'm sure you too yearn to touch once more. Like you, I'm having trouble passing to the Afterworld.'

Cora shook her head. 'I don't want to pass on. Not yet.'

Nancy Mittle turned back to Jake. 'Quite a trick with the sleeping bag. It fooled your father, and for a little while my sister and me . . .'

Jake blinked. 'What sleeping bag?' His eyes widened as he remembered it was only the previous evening he'd slipped from his dad's house, filling his sleeping bag with cushions to make it look like he was still asleep. 'Wait! You've been in my dad's house?'

She took a step towards him. 'A necessary evil – I personally thought we should give you the benefit of the doubt but my sister is made of sterner stuff than I.' She shrugged. 'And then you tried to kill the demon prince.'

'I was supposed to, but I didn't.' Jake paused. 'How did you know we were going to be here?'

'We have some understanding of how the prince's abilities work. It's not just the Afterworld's demonologist who studies the celestial beings. In fact, in demonology circles, his views are considered somewhat outdated.' She smiled. 'We knew you were with Cora and the prince, and we advised the Embassy to post Undoers at all sites on the Earthly Plane that you three have connections with. Luckily there were only a few possible locations, what with you, Jake, being so badly travelled.' She turned to Cora. 'And you were hardly out of St Bodelean's from the age of four.'

Cora gripped her hockey stick threateningly. 'Nancy, you have no physical form. You can't touch us. You can't harm us in any way.'

Jake scratched his head. Something was bothering him. 'If she has no presence how could she break a window?'

'She didn't,' came a voice. 'And Cora's right. She can't harm you.' Jake and Cora spun round to see the other Mittle sister, Agnes, blocking the entrance to the bathroom. She glowered at the children. 'But I can!'

Her sister looked at her with concern. 'Is the prince safe?'

Agnes nodded. 'He rests outside the door. He's low on energy but they haven't harmed him yet.'

Jake held his hands up. 'We're not trying to harm the prince. Or anyone for that matter. We're on your side. I promise. It's all a misunderstanding.'

'I'm afraid the Ambassador won't accept the word of someone she saw clutching the handle of the one knife that could send Prince Arkus to the

Eternal Void.' Agnes looked to her sister and then back to them. 'This ends now. You end now.'

Her ghostly sister clapped her hands. 'Daddy's legacy? Oh, please! Finally. It does seem rather apt.'

Agnes frowned. 'Don't be so silly, Nancy. We're doing this properly. We will summon Mawkins.'

Cora interrupted. 'Fortune won't give up. Even if we are sent to the Void. He'll still try to kill the prince. He wants to run the Afterworld Authorities without any demons.'

Nancy Mittle's mouth fell open. She seemed confused. 'Tokelo Fortune?'

'Tokelo Fortune . . . He wants the Afterworld Authorities to be free of demons so the dead – specifically him – can rule the Afterworld alone.'

Nancy Mittle's mouth opened wider. 'Tokelo Fortune is behind this? What nonsense.' She glanced across at her sister.

'It can't be, can it, Agnes?'

Agnes frowned. She looked at Cora. 'Continue . . .' she ordered.

'Finally . . .' Cora huffed. Then she started speaking. 'Tokelo Fortune told us that Arkus was a follower of

Fenris and that it was Jake's destiny to send him to the Void. But Jake couldn't – mainly because Jake's too cowardly – which was lucky because it turns out Arkus isn't a follower of Fenris at all.'

She took a deep breath and continued. 'Fortune wants to rule the Afterworld without demons. So even if you get rid of us, he'll still be there trying to get rid of Arkus. We're trying to get Arkus to safety. And if you're not going to help then we'll just have to do it without you. Even if it does mean Jake stays too long outside his body and dies. It's a sacrifice he's prepared to make.'

Jake started to speak but Cora wouldn't stop, cutting him off mid-protest.

'We're the good guys.' She jabbed a finger towards the sisters. 'How many times have you saved the world?' She looked at Jake then back at Nancy. '*I've* saved the world twice so far, with a bit of help from Jake, and I'll be damned if I'm going to let you stop us because you don't believe that Tokelo Fortune is trying to kill Arkus.'

'Enough!' The voice was a whisper but it had enough confidence and force to make the sisters start. It was Arkus. He was leaning against the doorframe.

Agnes dropped to a knee. 'Your Highness.' She bowed her head.

Arkus straightened up. He held a hand towards Jake. 'Jake is no kidnapper or assassin. It was he who saved me. He fought off the curse of the tooth. A lesser person may have succumbed to the dagger's power. What they say is the truth.'

The sisters looked at Jake. Then they looked at each other. Eventually Agnes spoke.

'This news is most perturbing. If Tokelo Fortune truly seeks to send Arkus to the Void . . .' Her eyes narrowed. 'We must indeed seek sanctuary in the Embassy of the Dead.'

'That's what we were trying to do before you found us,' said Jake.

'And it's lucky we did. The Ambassador will get to the bottom of your story. Perhaps I have misjudged you, Wormling. We'll ask the Embassy to recall Mawkins until your case has been heard.'

The younger sister smiled. 'Didn't I say, Agnes? You were always too quick to judge, weren't you?'

Agnes scowled. Then her face softened. 'We suspected your connection to Uthred as soon as we saw your initiation ceremony. "Wormling"– the young of a dragon. When news that you had found a tooth reached us we could be nearly certain. We crept into your house. Last night.' She took a knife from the folds of her clothes and tested the blade with her thumb. 'I was going to cut the tooth from you as you slept. Without it you posed no threat.' She looked down the blade. 'But you had gone . . .'

'We had top-secret business to attend to,' said Cora.

'Yes, you were going to Undo the bird-watcher's ghost.'

'So much for top secret,' muttered Cora.

Jake looked at his feet. 'Anyway, he turned out to be a Wandering Wight.' He shuddered at the memory. 'Someone switched the . . .' He stared at the sisters. 'It was you!'

The elder sister frowned. 'You must remember that until five minutes ago we thought you were destined to send the sole heir of the demon kingdom to the Eternal Void. Sending *you* to the Void would have neutralised your threat. It was a safety precaution. Just in case we failed to get the tooth. You were supposed to go the following day.'

'Well, it was partly because Mum's got better breakfast cereal than Dad and I didn't want to miss . . .' Jake was interrupted by the sound of the prince coughing. Jake looked at the sisters. 'You need to summon help from the Embassy at once. Can you do that?'

The elder sister placed the knife back in the folds of her dress and pulled out a box. Jake recognised it immediately.

'Hooray! A Mousephone!' he blurted out, excitedly, then added, 'I mean, a Necrommunicator. Good idea!'

He watched as Agnes opened the drawer and pushed a button. 'Hello?' she said to the dead mouse. 'Hello. Requesting urgent assistance.'

There was a pause. The mouse didn't move.

'Hello?' There was an edge of irritation to her voice. 'Hello?'

Still the mouse remained persistently inanimate.

Agnes looked at her sister. 'It's never not worked before.'

Cora sighed. 'That's happened to ours too,' she said. 'Tokelo Fortune disabled it. It was how he got us invited to the Embassy in time for the prince's visit. He said if he's close enough he can intercept or block the spirit transmission.'

Agnes looked at her. 'Tokelo?' She glanced nervously at the window. Outside the sun was beginning to set. 'We may have dallied too long. He must be close.'

Jake too looked to the big window in the main room. He could see the long single road winding its way through the tangled moorland, disappearing into the twilight. Something cut through the gloom – the headlights of a car, illuminating the windows.

Nancy wrung her hands and looked towards her sister. 'It looks like Tokelo Fortune has arrived. What should we do, Agnes?'

Agnes frowned. 'We need to get out of this place. And quickly . . .'

Cora held up her hockey stick. 'I'm ready to fight my way out!' she snarled.

A thought suddenly sprang into Jake's mind. 'Wait! The parcel . . .'

'Which one?'

Jake took his rucksack off and unzipped it. 'The package I picked up from Mum's!' He paused. 'I don't want to touch the dagger,' he mumbled.

Agnes nodded. 'That is wise. According to my research the dagger has the power to compel the Chosen One to act against his will. Its influence over you is lesser on the Earthly Plane but you won't be able to fight it every time. Sooner or later you will succumb.'

Jake groaned. 'I wish someone else could take it.'

Agnes looked at Cora. 'You try, child,' she said.

Cora stared at her. 'I have no presence. I can't hold anything apart from my hockey stick.'

'You haven't tried? It's a celestial object. You may have the power to grasp it.'

Cora reached into the bag and pulled out the dagger. 'I can hold it! It's like my hockey stick.' She smiled excitedly. 'Are you sure you don't mind, Jake?'

Jake swallowed hard. He felt weird about someone else holding the dagger with the tooth mounted inside. He took a deep breath. 'I don't want it. You keep it safe, Cora.'

Safe meant away from him.

Cora tucked it into the belt of her school dress. 'I will,' she said.

She handed the rucksack back to him.

Jake slapped his forehead. 'I'm such an idiot.'

He pulled out the package he'd picked up at his mum's house and showed it to the sisters.

'What is it?' asked Cora.

'Don't you remember?' said Jake, ripping the packaging open. He did his best impression of Wilkinson. 'The spectral postal service is very efficient in matters like this.' He put his hand inside and pulled out a box.

'A new Mousephone!' Nancy gasped.

'You call it a Mousephone too?' Jake laughed.

'Doesn't everybody? Necrommunicator is such a mouthful!'

Agnes growled. 'Enough. Make the call, boy!'

Jake slid the drawer of the Mousephone open and pressed the button. The mouse sat up sharply.

'Goodness me!' it declared in a small croaky voice. 'Is that you, Jake? Let me just finish reloading my stapler. Can't beat a spring-mounted Rexel Gazelle for fast loading.' They were the unmistakable words of Wilkinson. 'Where are you, Wormling? We've sent out Undoers to catch you both. You're in big trouble! I urge you to return to the Embassy at once. Awfully good to hear from you though, old chap. I rather thought I'd lost you.'

'I know, I know,' said Jake. 'Look, there's no time to explain. We're at Cora's parents' house. We have the prince. He's safe but very weak. Tokelo Fortune is trying to send him to the Void. Fortune wants to wipe out—'

The mouse interrupted. 'Wants to wipe out all demonkind?'

'You already know?' asked Jake, surprised. The words died in his throat. Something about the mouse's posture had changed. It was no longer sitting nervously upright in the box like Wilkinson at his desk. Instead it was leaning backwards, relaxed and calm, its arm curled around, in the position of someone holding his own head at his side.

'Tokelo Fortune wants to restore the Afterworld to its rightful owners – the dead?' continued the mouse tauntingly.

Jake gasped. They were no longer the words of Wilkinson. They were the words of Tokelo Fortune!

'I'm afraid I've intercepted your line of communication.' The mouse laughed. 'It's over. The prince will die by the hand of the Chosen One. It has been written since the passing of Uthred into the Void.'

Jake closed the box and stared at it. He felt the familiar shape of Zorro slink between his feet. He looked down at Zorro's snaggle-toothed face. 'We have to get out of here!'

Jake linked his arm with Arkus.

'Do you have enough energy to walk?' he asked.

Arkus nodded grimly.

Nancy's head appeared through the bathroom door. 'It's all quiet,' she whispered. 'We need to go. And quickly.'

The unlikely group followed Cora across the large open room towards a door.

'It leads to the hallway and the front door,' she explained as she pulled it open, then screamed and slammed it shut again as a dark shape leapt towards her. Too late. The creature was on her face. Cora fell back, her hockey stick clattering to the ground. It was the Gomseer! Its spindly legs were scrabbling for purchase, struggling with Cora's lack of physical form, pushing through her face, like it was trying to wade through water. But it was finding *something.* Something inside her head.

'Get it off me!' she screamed, writhing on the floor, clutching at the creature, her formless fingers passing helplessly through its body. Jake could see the creature unfurling its proboscis. He reached towards it, feeling a strange sudden coldness as his solid hand penetrated Cora's face, until he felt his fingers gripping the soft, warm body of the Gomseer. Gritting his teeth, he pulled it from her and, just as it whipped its proboscis towards his hand, he hurled it against the wall. Stunned, it slid to the ground at the feet of Agnes. She lifted her skirt slightly and brought a high-laced boot down upon the celestial creature. Jake felt vomit rising in his throat, as the creature's abdomen ruptured beneath her boot, oozing brown liquid across the floor.

The Gomseer was dead.

Cora, still lying on her back, blinked up at Jake. 'Thanks, Precious, but I was coping just fine.' She reached for her hockey stick and sprang to her feet. 'Let's go.'

She opened the door again.

This time Jake was close enough to see over her shoulder. Another Gomseer had squeezed through – flattening its soft body to fit through the letter box. As he watched another followed. And another.

'There's more than one.' He groaned. 'I thought there was only one!'

Jake watched one of the Gomseers scuttle up the wall where it disappeared into a dark patch of what he'd initially thought was shadow.

He blinked. It wasn't a shadow at all. It was a group of the soul-sucking spider-things, huddling together. 'There's a *lot* more than one!'

Cora closed the door. 'Maybe not this way, Precious.'

Agnes frowned. 'They'll be forcing their way into all the ground-floor entrances.' She looked at Cora. 'Is there a way out, one from high up?'

Cora paused for a second. 'Upstairs. The window

in my room! We can climb down from it on to the first-floor roof and go out that way. I used to do it all the time when Father tried to stop me going to hockey practice.'

Jake led the hobbling Arkus up the stairs, following Cora, Zorro and Nancy.

But Nancy had stopped. 'Agnes, dear. What are you doing?'

Agnes looked up at her ghost sister. 'Nancy, take the children to safety,' she said. She looked at Jake. 'You just have to stay alive long enough for the Embassy of the Dead to arrive . . . If Wilkinson has sent them.'

Jake exchanged a glance with Cora.

It seemed like a big *if.*

Agnes reached into the folds of her dress and pulled out her knife. Silver flashed in the air. Then she faced the door.

'This way!' cried Cora from the top of the stairs. 'You can climb out my bedroom window.' She disappeared through a door.

Jake opened it behind her, and helped the prince through.

Cora had paused in the middle of the room. She was looking around. 'It's changed a bit since I was alive.'

Jake looked around as well. 'This explains everything,' he said.

At some point Cora's bedroom had been converted to a trophy room. The packing had only just begun in here. A stack of unconstructed cardboard boxes leant against the far wall.

Jake surveyed a shelf. All sorts of triumphs recorded in certificates and silver trophies were lined up, proclaiming the name 'Arthur Sanderford'. Jake looked at Cora. 'These are *all* your dad's?'

'Yup.' She pushed her head through the pane of the window. 'It's all clear outside. I think. But it looks like the window's locked.'

Jake sat Arkus against a wall. He ran to the window and tried to pull it open. 'It's locked. Where's the key?'

'I have no idea. Smash it with that medal case.'

Jake took a frame from the wall. Inside it, encased in glass, was a medal. 'Is this a knighthood?'

'No, it's the Order of the British Empire, an OBE.

Father's knighthood is over there. Just smash the glass, Precious.'

Jake lifted the frame above his head. Something on the opposite wall caught his eye.

Cora sighed. 'Yes, it is an Olympic medal. It's actually Mother's. She won it sailing at Mexico '82. Not that Father noticed.'

It was beneath a framed picture of a boat surging through the waves.

'I've seen that boat somewhere . . .' Jake said.

'It's the one outside. After Mother died Father just left it to rot.'

Jake nodded. 'Weird how I recognised it from the ruins outside,' he said, more to himself than to Cora. In the photo it was coursing through the water, shiny white hull glistening in the sunlight. The boat outside was covered in green algae and sat in the muddy shallows, tilted to one side. A rotting spectre of its former self.

Cora looked at him. 'Stop daydreaming. We're in a rush to save the world, remember!'

Jake hurled the framed OBE at the window. It bounced off and narrowly missed rebounding into his face. Something fell from the wooden window frame. A key. Jake picked it up and tried it in the lock. It clicked.

'That was my plan all along,' said Cora. 'Open the window then, Precious.'

The window slid open seamlessly, and the cold night air hit his face.

Suddenly, Nancy burst through the wall of the room. Jake barely had time to let out a short squeal of fright.

'There's rather a lot of those horrid creatures down there!' She glanced at her watch. 'We have one minute.'

'One minute till what?' asked Cora.

Nancy smiled mischievously. 'Daddy's special legacy!'

'What is that? Will Agnes be OK?'

A brief flash of sadness passed over Nancy's face. 'Agnes will find a way to stay alive. She's rather good at that.' She forced a smile and motioned to the window. 'After you,' she said.

Cora was first out of the window. Or rather, she glided through the wall. Zorro didn't need any encouragement. He leapt through the window on to the flat first-floor roof.

Jake climbed through after him with considerably less agility. He turned and, using all his strength, heaved Arkus through after him.

'How are you doing?' he asked the prince.

Arkus looked at him and smiled weakly.

'This way!' cried Cora. In the time it had taken Jake to heave Arkus over the roof, she'd already descended to the ground. Now her face peeked over the edge. Jake helped Arkus over. Cora was standing on a large, old compost heap that was piled against the back of the house. The moon was now in the sky, and the lake glittered in its soft light.

Jake lowered the prince, dropped down after him and then dragged him away from the house. Nancy Mittle was waiting.

'Ten seconds,' she said, looking at her wristwatch. 'At least, I think there are still ten seconds left before Daddy's special legacy actually—'

THE BATHROOM

The explosion knocked Jake from his feet. He felt the heat on his skin. He felt the fragments of exploding concrete and glass pepper his body. He felt the cloying thick smoke in his mouth and throat.

KABOOM

The smoke was so thick Jake couldn't see anything. He reached out into the darkness.

'Arkus?'

'Jake!' The voice was weak but close. 'Here, Jake.'

Jake stumbled through the smoke towards the lake and the voice. The ground was strewn with debris from the house. He found Arkus on the beach of the lake, next to the remains of an expensive-looking grandfather clock embedded in the shingle.

'Are you OK?'

Arkus nodded. 'Me and Zorro are fine.'

Zorro was cringing behind the prince. He'd bolted at the sound of the explosion even though he couldn't be hurt.

Cora approached through the settling smoke. She looked at Jake.

'They're both doing better than my house. There goes my inheritance.'

Jake scratched his head. 'I'm no legal expert but I'm pretty sure the dead don't get to be in the will.'

Jake looked back at the shell of Cora's parents' burning house.

The ghostly form of Nancy Mittle was disappearing into the smoke.

'Agnes?' he asked. 'Where is she? We need to go back . . .'

Cora frowned. She pointed to a small outbuilding a hundred yards or so away on the edge of the lake. 'Mother's boathouse. We'll meet there. You go with Arkus. I'll help look for Agnes.'

Jake shook his head. 'No. I'll go back for her. She might need help. I'm the only one with a physical presence.' He looked at Arkus. 'Can you make it to that building?'

Arkus grimaced. 'I can but try.'

Jake glanced at Cora. 'I'll meet you there. Look after him. Tokelo Fortune may be close.'

Cora nodded and her hockey stick materialised

in her hands. She held it up threateningly. 'You bet I will,' she snarled.

Jake shielded his eyes from the heat of the burning building. In the dim glow of sunset the light from the flames danced across the scrub, and the smoke hung heavy to the ground. Through the smoke he saw Nancy change direction as if she had seen something. Something smoking. Something that seemed to have been hurled from the house in the explosion. He followed Nancy away from the building and the boathouse, to the old jetty jutting out ten or so metres into the lake. A smouldering heap lay on the rotten planks.

By the time he'd run to the jetty Nancy was kneeling by the heap. It was clothes. Clothes and something else. The acrid scent of burning hair hung heavy in the air, and Jake realised the heap was Agnes Mittle. She was curled on the mossy planks, her eyes staring wildly into the sky, her long, grey hair singed at the ends and her face covered in soot. Her spectral sister, Nancy, crouched in front of her.

'Agnes, darling? Can you hear me?'

Agnes blinked. 'Did we get them all? Did we get those horrid spiders?'

Nancy looked back at the burning building. A flaming timber crashed to the ground in a shower of sparks. She nodded. 'You did, darling, you did.'

Agnes looked at Jake. Her eyelashes were clogged with soot. 'You're a good boy, Jake.'

'Thank you,' he whispered.

A thin smile spread across her lips. 'Daddy's special legacy . . .' she muttered. Then she raised her arms from the floor, mimicking an explosion. 'Kaboom!' She closed her eyes.

Jake looked around, nervously. 'We need to get you out of here. Tokelo Fortune is close. If we can just get far enough away from him we might be able to use our Mousephones to contact the Embassy and an ambulance for . . .' He stopped.

Nancy was looking at Agnes. He watched as she tried to brush a strand of grey hair from her sister's forehead. Her fingers passed straight through. 'She's dead,' she said, not looking up. 'Agnes is dead.'

Jake bit his lip.

Nancy reached out to him but her hand passed

through his shoulder. 'Don't be sad. She and I will be together now . . . in the Afterworld.' She smiled. 'Make sure it's still running smoothly by the time we arrive.'

'How are you getting there?' asked Jake. And then he realised. Nancy was slowly disappearing, a happy smile spread across her face.

'She's been Undone!' he whispered to himself as he understood.

All this time spent haunting the Earthly Plane she had been waiting for her sister. Even in death, it seemed, they could not be apart.

Jake stood and looked at the body of Agnes. In life she had been a strong woman. In death she looked old – old but peaceful.

He looked towards the wreck of the burning house. Agnes had sacrificed herself to save them from the Gomseers and she had succeeded. Now it was up to him to get the prince to the safety of the Embassy. But someone else was emerging from the smoke. A man, standing at the end of the jetty, blocking Jake's path back on to the shore.

It was Tokelo Fortune.

DEATH

'Hello, Wormling.' Fortune smiled at Jake from beneath his arm. 'I wasn't expecting Agnes' pyrotechnic display. She wiped out all of my little pets.' A fat, round spider-creature crawled on to his shoulder and nestled against his head. 'Apart from one.'

Tokelo took a pace forward and Jake instinctively stepped backwards, tripping over the top of a supporting post that projected through the jetty. He twisted as he fell, feeling a flash of pain as his hand smashed through the rotten wood and his chin scraped down against the planks. His face hung over the edge of the jetty and for a second he gasped at his faint reflection staring back at him, distorted by the ripples in the water, like his own ghost twin. Despite the darkness, he could see beneath the structure on which he lay. The rest of the wooden post that he'd tripped over was holding one side of the jetty up. It was rotten.

He scrabbled round and sat up. Tokelo was nearer, halfway down the jetty towards him. He raised a hand and the last Gomseer crawled from his shoulder down to his palm. 'Before the night is over Arkus will be sent to the Eternal Void and the dead will rule the Afterworld alone.' Tokelo smiled. 'That's the thing with destinies . . . They have a habit of being fulfilled. Even if it is in the most unexpected way!'

Jake looked up. 'The demonologist said only I can send Arkus to the Void. And I'm definitely not going to.' He blinked as the Gomseer uncurled its proboscis. 'Especially if I'm a withered husk.'

Tokelo smiled. 'Maybe there's been a mistake.' He stepped forward once more, lowering his hand towards the wooden boards, and as he did so the Gomseer prepared to pounce.

Jake repositioned himself slightly, and kicked out. A look of sudden confusion crossed Fortune's face as Jake's foot made contact with the top of the wooden post. The expression turned to dismay as the post split from its holding, the nails tearing easily from the rotten wood, and one side of the jetty collapsed into the freezing lake. For a second, Tokelo teetered on the edge, and then his foot lost its grip and he tumbled, his head falling from his shoulders as his body smashed against the side of the jetty, and fell into the lake. His head rolled towards Jake, and instinctively Jake put a hand out to stop it tumbling into the lake too.

Now Jake sat on the end of a wrecked jetty with the head of Tokelo Fortune, and the last Gomseer.

Tokelo's eyes flicked to Jake, and then back to his pet. 'Finish him!' the head commanded.

The Gomseer pounced. Jake grabbed the only object that was in reach – Tokelo's head – and shielded himself from the proboscis as it whipped through the air towards him.

He opened his eyes.

In his hands was the spectral head of the Minister of Security, and latched to the head was the engorged body of the Minister's own pet Gomseer that was now sucking the spirit energy from Tokelo's face. As the Gomseer slowly swelled, so Tokelo Fortune's head shrivelled, and for a second Jake was holding what seemed like the head of an ancient Tokelo Fortune. Then it was just dust – flowing through his fingers and catching the breeze, floating out over the lake.

The Gomseer lay on the floor, bloated and lazy. Jake stood up cautiously, and flicked the creature away with his foot, back on to the shore.

He watched as the Gomseer slowly recurled its proboscis. It was just beginning to clean itself when a figure emerged from the darkness and crushed the creature beneath a familiar-looking riding boot.

Jake's gaze moved slowly upwards. Above the riding boots was a pair of jodhpurs. Above the jodhpurs was a riding jacket, and above the jacket was the face of a very stern-looking woman. It was the Ambassador of the Embassy of the Dead.

Jake gulped.

The Ambassador wiped her boot on the jetty. 'Luckily for you, Wilkinson received just enough of your message to let us know where you were. It seems Minister Fortune has been up to no good . . .' She looked Jake up and down. 'So, you were the Chosen

One . . . And you had the strength to fight off the influence of the demon-slayer's tooth. It is supposed to be extremely difficult for the Chosen One to resist its corrupting powers.'

'That's why I gave it to Cora to look after.'

The Ambassador looked around. 'And where is Prince Arkus? I trust he is safe.'

Jake nodded towards the boathouse. 'He's with Cora in there . . . He's weak but still with us.'

The Ambassador sighed with relief. 'The power of the tooth has been thwarted.' She looked at him. 'Destiny called but there was no answer.'

Jake wasn't listening. Something Tokelo had said was ringing in his ears.

Maybe there's been a mistake.

'Why did he try to kill me?' he wondered aloud.

The Ambassador frowned. 'What do you mean?'

'Why would Tokelo try to kill the one person who could kill Arkus?'

The Ambassador looked thoughtful. 'Maybe he realised the game was up? Maybe he just wanted revenge for you foiling his plot?'

Jake shook his head. 'He said Arkus would die

tonight.' He paused. Behind the Ambassador the rotten remains of the boat lay half beached on the shore. It was weird that he'd recognised the photo of Cora's mum's boat from this rotten wreck.

Then he realised that he *hadn't*.

He'd recognised the boat in the photo from somewhere else.

He'd recognised it from the model boat in his vision! The broken boat. It was *incredibly* similar to Cora's mum's boat – the boat that now sat, listing on the lake. He stepped off the jetty into the cold of the water. Once, long ago, the name of the boat had been hand-painted on the hull. Now time and decay had erased all but the first letter. *U.* The rest of the name may have peeled away but it had left a faint memory of the letters that had once been there, in a slightly darker green.

U. T. H. R. E. D.

The name of the demon-slayer. Jake's ancestor. He scratched his head.

No way was that just a coincidence.

Why would Cora's mum call a boat after an ancient Viking? Her dad had been a professor of Nordic history . . . And hadn't Cora said she recognised the word Uthred? It wasn't from her lessons. It was the name of her mum's boat.

Maybe her dad had named it?

It was at times like this he needed Cora. Instinctively he reached for his jeans pocket to fetch his phone to call her before realising he neither had his phone nor did Cora *ever* have one.

He looked at his empty left hand. Then it hit him. When he had held the dagger in real life, it had felt like part of him, an extension of his hand. In his vision something had felt odd about how he'd been holding the dagger. It had felt strange and alien.

In the vision he had been holding the dagger in his right hand!

Jake was left-handed!

He couldn't even use a pair of scissors right-handed, let alone administer a fatal blow to the prince of demons.

The Ambassador frowned at him. 'What is it, Jake?'

Jake blinked.

The assassin in the vision wasn't me.

He slapped his forehead. He'd had visions before – and they hadn't ever been about himself – always from the perspective of other people. He swore under his breath. He'd just accepted that he was the Chosen One. He'd just accepted that the vision was of him.

You always assume it's all about you, Jake.

That's what Cora had said.

And she was right!

He felt sick as the fragments of the broken prophecy fell into place.

He looked at the Ambassador. 'It wasn't *my* destiny . . . I'm not the heir of Uthred Dragon. In my vision it wasn't my actions I was seeing. It was someone else's. At some point Tokelo must have realised this. That's why he believed the prophecy would still happen even if he killed me . . .'

The Ambassador looked at him sharply. 'If you're not the Chosen One, then who is?'

'It's Cora! Cora is the Chosen One!'

The Ambassador stared at him. 'My God, child! She's got the dagger and the tooth.'

He nodded grimly. 'And the prince.'

THE BOATHOUSE

J ake pushed open the door to the boathouse so fast that he nearly fell through it. It opened out on to a covered inlet of deep water. Once, before it was left outside to rot, Cora's mum's boat would have moored here, safe from the harsh weather. A walkway edged around the inlet of water, leading out into a small room. Arkus was leaning against the wooden walls, using them to support his weight. A figure stood between him and Jake.

It was Cora. Her back was to Jake and she was holding the knife.

Arkus's eyes flashed across the water. *I'm scared,* he mouthed.

Cora took a step towards the prince. 'All Sanderfords achieve great things.'

'Cora!' called out Jake.

She stopped. Without looking around she started to speak. 'Can't you see, I'm busy fulfilling *my* destiny, Precious? It's me. I'm the Chosen One. The tooth has found the heir.'

'It's just a prophecy,' shouted Jake. He began to edge towards her. 'Put down the knife.'

Cora shook her head. 'I always knew I was destined for something great . . . Like my father. Like my ancestor, Uthred.' She turned her head slightly. 'It's only just come to me, though . . . Father was obsessed with his ancestry. That's why he became a professor of history. I remembered the day he gave Mother the boat. A birthday present. He couldn't resist naming it after his favourite historical person. His ancestor . . . Uthred. I knew I'd heard that name before.' For a moment she paused and her eyes took on a softer, more familiar look. 'Mother loved that boat. She even had a model made of it after she won her medal . . . Look.' She pointed to a table beside Arkus. On it sat the boat from Jake's vision. It was unbroken.

Cora took a step closer to Arkus and he tried to move away from her. His fingers gripped the wall to hold himself up, but he slipped and fell hard against the table, collapsing to the floor, and bringing the model boat with him. It smashed as it hit the ground. Arkus lay amongst its shattered remains, his body covered by his cloak.

For a moment the three of them were silent and then Arkus spoke in a broken voice, words Jake had heard for the first time just that morning. '*Today my final battle will be fought, but tomorrow my heir will rise and he shall bear the tooth trophy of Uthred Dragon, the demon-slayer. The lineage of demon kings shall be ended for all time.*' He looked up at Jake with terror in his eyes. 'The prophecy. The prophecy is coming true.'

Cora laughed. But it didn't sound like her real laugh. She held the knife aloft, gazing at the tooth set into its hilt. '*He* shall bear the toothed trophy.' She turned to look at Jake. 'He? Do you see? Didn't the Mittle sisters say that the demonologist's views were considered somewhat outdated?'

Jake frowned. 'I don't understand.'

Cora rolled her eyes. 'He said himself that early dead scholars of the Afterworld excised all mention of women from the original chronicles of Afterworld history, apportioning their triumphs to their male counterparts.' She laughed. 'It didn't occur to the demonologist that it might have also been the case with the prophecy. They all presumed it was about you because you found the tooth . . . you were the one they assumed was the hero. Because you were the boy. And they were all men! But *actually* it was about me.'

Jake didn't know what to say. She was right.

'I . . . I found it, though,' he said.

'You only found the tooth because it was trying to find *me*.' She giggled. 'It's all been about *me*. That's why Tokelo was smiling as I disappeared from the Afterworld. He had realised who I was. After I told him my father had traced our family back to Viking times.'

She held the dagger before her eyes, as if speaking directly to it. 'And now I will finally live up to the Sanderford name. The Afterworld shall for ever be ruled by the dead. And I shall be known as the greatest Sanderford of all.' She smiled. 'How do you like that, Father?'

Jake no longer recognised his friend. Everything about her had changed. Her face seemed sunken, her eyes rimmed with red. She faced Arkus and readied the knife.

'Wait!' said Jake. His voice was steady and calm. 'You don't have to do this. You can put the knife down and we can all just go home.'

'Home?' she spat. 'I don't have a home. Not this burning wreck . . . Not St Bodelean's. Nowhere . . .'

Jake shook his head. 'But you do have a home. With me. That's your home. That's all a home is . . . Somewhere you're safe and people love you . . .'

He took a step forward. 'You don't have to do this.'

Cora paused. 'It is my destiny . . .'

'It's not. Don't you see? We choose our own destinies. Every one of us . . .'

'It's not like that for me, Jake,' she replied. 'Maybe it's like that for people like you. Normal people . . . But I've been chosen . . .' Jake heard her voice cracking. 'It's what I must do. For my father. For my ancestors.'

Jake took another step forward. 'It's all make-believe. Say no one had realised that you were the

Chosen One. Say it was still me. And I did it. I carried out the deed. Wouldn't everyone be saying . . .' He put on a silly voice. '"The prophecy has been fulfilled."'

Cora lifted the knife higher.

Jake continued, speaking fast. '*You're* choosing to do this . . . You're making this your fate, your destiny, whatever you want to call it. But it doesn't have to be this way.'

'I must see my destiny through.'

'You just need to make the right decision, Cora.' Jake felt his voice breaking. 'Make the decision that Cora Sanderford would make. Not the decision your dad would make, or the decision Uthred Dragon would make.' He felt tears welling in his eyes. 'You need to make your own choice!'

'This is my choice!' She spat the words but there was something in her voice. Something that gave him hope.

He looked at her. 'I don't believe you. I don't believe that Cora Sanderford needs to do anything, for anybody.' He lowered his voice to a barely audible whisper. 'Not the Cora Sanderford I know, anyway.'

The knife was high in the air. Cora's hand loosened its grip and for a second it balanced between her fingers before it fell, the tooth dropping from its niche and skidding across the floor. Cora looked at Jake, wide-eyed. 'I'm free,' she gasped. 'I'm free of my father and of Uthred, and of everybody. I'm free to be Cora Sanderford.'

Jake rushed past and lifted Arkus from the floor. He groaned in pain.

'Are you OK?' asked Jake.

'I'll be fine, Jake. Thank you.'

Cora blinked. 'What just happened?'

Jake looked up to see the Ambassador stoop and pick up the tooth. She looked at it closely and turned it around in her fingers.

'You've both just saved the Afterworld,' she said.

Cora blinked a second time. 'Again?'

The Ambassador smiled proudly. 'Yes. Simply by having the strength to fight against those who sought to force your destiny into the one they wished for themselves. You've defied the prophecy. You've shown your spirit to be stronger than Uthred Dragon himself.'

She turned to Jake. 'And you too. A surprising amount of wisdom in one so outwardly lacking in gumption.'

Jake frowned. 'Thank you . . .' he said. 'I think.'

Cora looked at Jake. 'I saved the Afterworld . . .' she repeated, sounding a little dazed. Then she straightened her boater. 'That's three times now.'

The Ambassador nodded at Jake. 'Your assistant has shown herself to be strong in the face of danger . . .' She smiled at Cora. 'And perhaps in the shedding of your supposed destiny you have learnt a powerful lesson. Powerful enough to finally break the bond that holds you to the Earthly Plane, perhaps?'

Cora gripped her hockey stick. 'You mean Jake's Undone me?' She looked at Jake. 'I'm passing on?'

Jake was suddenly aware of his heart beating. There was so much he needed to say. He hadn't known Cora long but the thought of never seeing his friend again wasn't the best feeling, to say the least. He swallowed. 'Are you sure? Do you feel anything, Cora?' He looked at the Ambassador. 'Shouldn't she have gone by now? Maybe she's not going . . .' He could hear the desperation in his own voice.

The Ambassador sniffed. 'Sometimes, when the tether to the Earthly Plane has been strong, the process takes a little longer. We should know within the minute.'

Cora looked at Jake, and took a deep breath. 'Look, Precious. If I am going to pass on there's something I'd like to say . . .'

She paused. 'What's that weird smell of ham?'

'Ham?' asked Jake. Then he remembered the way Zorro was to be called back by Eustace.

He looked at his cloakroom ticket. It said five. He looked at Cora. 'Go on,' he urged as Zorro suddenly disappeared. 'Quickly. Eustace is calling us back.'

She smiled. 'I guess I owe you a—'

Just before Jake got to hear what might have been the first ever thank you or apology coming from Cora's mouth, he felt the ice-cold shock of freezing water splashing in his face. He wiped his eyes and he was back in his bedroom, and back in his body.

Eustace and Sab were looking at him. Zorro was poking his transparent nose through a slice of ham that had been laid on his pillow in what seemed like some kind of weird ceremony.

Eustace gazed at him. 'Thank goodness, Jake. You're back . . . And not a moment too soon. Your body was beginning to look a little peaky.'

Jake wiped the wet hair away from his eyes, looking around desperately for his friend. 'Cora!' he cried. 'She might have been Undone!'

Sab was still holding an empty bucket. 'Undone? You mean she's passed to the Afterworld?'

Jake stood up and took off his rucksack. He unzipped it and pulled out Cora's trophy. Its lid was still wedged open. 'That's just it. I don't know for sure. There's only one way to find out!'

He placed Cora's trophy in the middle of the floor, closed the lid and waited.

W ill Mabbitt has an overactive imagination. It used to get him in trouble, but now it's his job. His first book, *The Unlikely Adventures of Mabel Jones*, was shortlisted for the Branford Boase Award. He's achieved little else of note, preferring to spend his time loitering in graveyards looking for ideas. He lives with his family on the south coast of England.

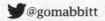 @gomabbitt